This book is a work of fiction. All characters, names, locations, and events portrayed in this book are fictional or used in an imaginary manner to entertain, and any resemblance to any real people, situations, or incidents is purely coincidental.

A GUIDE TO FOLKTALES IN FRAGILE DIALECTS

Catherynne M. Valente

Copyright © 2008 by Catherynne M. Valente

Introduction Copyright © 2008 by Midori Snyder

All Rights Reserved.

Cover Art:
"Kitsune," Copyright © 2008 by Connie Toebe

Cover Design Copyright © 2008 by Mike Allen, Anita Allen, and David Zimet

ISBN-13: 978-1-934648-35-3
ISBN-10: 1-934648-35-3

Trade Paperback

May 31, 2008

A Publication of
Norilana Books
P. O. Box 2188
Winnetka, CA 91396
www.norilana.com

Printed in the United States of America

A Guide to Folktales in Fragile Dialects

Curiosities

an imprint of
Norilana Books

www.norilana.com

A Guide to Folktales in Fragile Dialects

Catherynne M. Valente

Introduction
by
Midori Snyder

For Danielle, A.E.M., S.J., Kat, and all my sisters, many and dear.

INTRODUCTION

by Midori Snyder

Catherynne M. Valente is one of the most inventive young writers in the modern mythic arts movement. She is an accomplished story teller and a master of language, especially those poetic dialects spoken by the women in *A Guide to Folktales in Fragile Dialects*. There is a gentle irony in the title for there is nothing fragile about the rich, organic language of these poems, their images deeply rooted in the senses and in nature. Here Rapunzel grows into the wild rampion of her origin, a fox wife wears two skins, a housebound woman evolves slowly into a tree, and an abusive husband transforms into a taloned crow. The seven devils of California push up from the land into the bodies of immigrants, leaving behind the taste of salt, sage, gold, sulfur, and iron.

Each one of these familiar (and often violent) tales is inscribed on a woman's body. Persephone suffers decay and rebirth in an eternal tug of war, blood flows unquenched from a maiden's mouth at her wedding altar, and a silent sister, savaged by abuse, continues with "flax-lashed hands" to restore humanity to her brothers. In Valente's re-telling of ancient stories we hear dark truths whispered beneath the skin of the tale. Cinderella slices the flesh from her sister's foot that she may fit the glass slipper and take Cinderella's place; a haunted Helen of Troy writhes with poison, hoping it will liberate her from the traumatic memories of war, and Bluebeard's last wife capitulates to an endless cycle of brutality.

But we also hear the strong voices of resistance and of experience. Sita, Goddess of the Ramayana who survived intact an ordeal by fire, contrasts her tale of empowerment to the failure of Persephone to reclaim her own life in the battle between Hades and Demeter. We hear the story of two sisters, the woman of iron and the woman of wood, each lost to the other, until an act of courage reconciles and brings them together again. And finally, we hear the authoritative voice of Baba Yaga herself, now an aging immigrant in a new country re-named "Barbara Young," teaching a modern young woman (and indeed, all of us) the fragile dialects of the past.

Midori Snyder
April 2008

The Girl with Two Skins

I.

On your knees between moon-green shoots,
beside a sack of seed, a silver can, a white spade,
a ball is tucked into the bustle of your skirt:
like a pearl
but not a pearl.
You pulled it up
round as a beet from between the mint and the beans
where I had sunk it in the earth,
as though I fished
for loam-finned, moss-gilled coelacanth
at the bottom of the world.
I thought it safe.

I crawl to you on belly henna-bright,
teeth out,
scratching the basil sprouts—
eyes flash phosphor. In the late light,
slant gold light,
you must see
the old tail echo
beneath my muddy dress:
two, three, nine.

I howl against the barking churchbells:
Give it back, give it back,
I need it.

II.

Once I skulked snoutwise through scrap-iron forests,
And to each man with his silver pail scowled:

You are not beautiful enough
to make me human.

I had a fox's education:
rich coffee grounds in every house-gutter,
mice whose bones were sweet to suck,
stolen bread and rainwater on whiskers:
slow theogonies of bottle-caps and housecats.

I crouched, the color of rusted stairs,
and to each boy who chased me
through rotted wheat laughed:

You are not beautiful enough
to turn my tail to feet!

But this is a story,
and in a story
there is always someone
beautiful enough.

In a wood I found you
in the classical way,
a girl in a dress with a high hem,
ribbons in her teeth,
honey on her thumbs.

(Damn all of you. All your red hair
just enough like fur,
Damn all your small mouth,
your damp smell,
Damn all your pianos and stitching hoops.
Had I but paws enough to stamp out
your every spoken word like snow!)

You spooled out lessons

like an older sister:
Make your waist like this,
indicating curve.
Make your eyes like this,
indicating blue.
Make your face
make your skin
make your clever, clever hands,
make them this way,
indicating civilized,
indicating soft, your own,
your freckled breast linen-bound.

The old vixens, with their scabby,
mushroom-strung claws,
only said to run from boys,
and you looked so thick and pure,
like the inside
of a bone.

III.

I lashed my tail to my waist
in your gold-wood kitchen,
ridiculous in blue silk,
with cornflowers in my ears.
We bent over squash soup and sour cherries,
you put your hands over mine
to show me how to crease dough
over a silver pan.
I bit your cheek at tea-time;
you smelled all day of my musk.

No, you laughed like sugar stirring,
your feet are too black,
your teeth are so sharp!

Can you not stand up straight
in my old dresses?
Can you not make your flesh
like mine?

Shamed, fur flamed across my cheek,
but you patted it pale with flour and sweet,
and I wept to be savage and bristle-stiff
in such a tidy place,
in such silent, clean arms.

I slept curled
at the foot of your bed,
reeking of lavender and lilac
though I spied no purple field.
I growled at moths that plagued your hair
and woke with every stairwell-creak.

But you brushed back my pelt
with lullabies,
into a long braid that fell
across pillows like shoulder blades.
You showed me the word *kitsune*
in a book with a long ribbonmark
like blood spilled on the print—
I chewed the page and swallowed it,
and learned there only that
crawling into your arms,
embarrassed by my heat, my wet nose,
was like becoming
a girl with two skins.

IV.

This is a story,
and it is true of all stories

that the sound when they slam shut
is like a key turning.

I was sewing, hands two bloody half-paws—
it takes such a long time to
become a woman—
smears of needle-bitten skin,
and you scrutinizing the cross-stitching:
no, no, like this, my love, like mine—
when he came to call, when you
with hair sleek as linseed oil
and my eyes still so black,
still unable to imitate the blue you demanded,
danced with him in our kitchen,
fed him our yellow soups with sprigs of thyme.

He smiled at me, with pomade in that grin,
and walking canes, and silverware,
and spring gloves. I snapped at him,
for a simple fox may still understand her rival,
and know what is expected.

But the recoil! The shrieking of her
the shrinking into his great smooth arms,
the lifting of her blue skirts to keep them clear
of the stink of my fume!

A vixen chews out the throat of her enemies
like stripping bark from a birch;
it is the sophisticated thing.
How was I to know you meant to keep him?

Absurd in my torn dress,
tail bulging free, the muzzle
you tried so to train to lips,
curled back, knife-whiskered,

I stood with blood beating my flesh to drum-taut,
in our kitchen, in our hall,
mange-sodden and mud-bellied,
before the man who was
beautiful enough,
beautiful enough.

V.

It is not possible, you said later,
when I scrabbled at the door he built,
when my skin was blue and bruised,
and there was no russet left in me,
when my nakedness in the snow
was goosepimpled and smelled so damp,
so much like soup
and cherries
and creased dough in a silver pan—
it is not possible to love for long
what is not a girl, sweet nor soft,
nor civilized,
nor trained to tile and mantle-shine,
stray beast in the house,
scolded when she spoils supper
with her hunger,
when her rough tongue spoils
every cultivated thing,
skin and sewing and lavender bed together.

See how tall he stands.
See how gentle his voice.
See how his hands on me never cut.

Then give it back,
I need it,
my pearl

which is not a pearl.
I do not want your shape.
Let me go back
I want to go back.

But you keep it by you,
pretty jeweled thing,
it adorns you as I did not.
The heat of you
warms it like an egg.

I am cold in this evening of blue chastenings,
I haunt your garden,
your raspberry rows,
your squash blossoms,
a naked wastrel,
flat teeth chattering.
I hold one arm out to you,
clung with snail-tracked ruin,
keep one over my breasts,
which you taught to be modest.

As the moon comes up
like a pearl,
but not a pearl,
you gather up the mint and rosemary,
and do not see
how I claw with woman's nails
the waist you gave me,
just to make it red again.

Tale Type 7307:
The Maiden who Bled at the Altar

In certain mountainous regions where a particular species of fern is found, whose leaves are serrated and a striking shade of gold, and the practice of mouse-herding has been perfected, there is a story which may only be told by the youngest daughters of a family. Transmission is therefore from child to child and variations are extreme.

The tale goes that a maiden, naturally the youngest of her clan, was so beautiful that the moon coughed when she was born, or descended to lay beside her in her cradle, or killed himself outright in despair of ever possessing her. This maiden was swaddled from the earliest age in the golden ferns of the highest crags, and men of every tribe sought to secure her in marriage, even before she could speak, or as soon as she could speak, or pressed her so severely that the child was too terrified to learn to speak. Finally, seeking solace from her many suitors, the child took refuge in the darkest of the mountain caves. There she played in the dank water and was happy until suppertime. After seven days, or seven moons, or as soon as she entered the darkest cave, she met a pale young boy her own age, or a tall pale warrior with ferns in his hair, or a stooped old grandfather with pale eyebrows. The youth, or the man, or the old wizard courted her, and she herself grew paler and paler when she returned home for suppertime. Her playmate led her further and further into the mountains until the girl was lost, and could not return home at all. The boy, or the warrior, or the grandfather, married her in the heart of the mountain with a bat as officiate. But when she went to kneel before her nuptial altar, the maiden began to bleed from the mouth, and bled and bled until the caves were awash in her blood. The pale man danced in her blood, and filled great stone goblets with it for the wedding feast, and wherever he touched it her blood became great dark rubies. The girl waltzed with him, stumbling, still coughing blood into the dark. Finally, she stripped off her dress of golden ferns and stuffed the sharp leaves into her mouth to staunch the flow, though it hurt her. But she could not breathe with her throat full of ferns, and fell down dead. The pale man cut her into six pieces and married each of them in turn below the milky eyes of the bat. He spent one night each with her arms, her legs, her torso and her head, whispering to them of love in the shadows, and the maiden whose beauty caused the moon such distress became the many wives of the emperor of the mountains.

Often, the maiden remains in this state, and offers instruction in the delicacies of plural marriage to young girls whose mouse-herds are still small. However, a Swedish anthropologist heard from the ninth daughter of the mouse-king, whose eyes seemed to him fierce and feral in the dark, that the head of the fern-maiden conspired with the bat-priest, and he carried her by the hair to each of her other limbs, and she sewed herself back together, learned rudimentary echolocation from the patient bat, and walked straight and tall out of the darkest caves. She found that much time had passed, and all her suitors had died. New ones were not forthcoming, as the maiden was now badly scarred and blind, and so she was left alone, and led a very happy life as a mouse-witch, and never married anyone, ever.

According to the twelfth daughter of a one-legged herdsman, who was then very small indeed, the maiden never made it so far as all that, and is still bleeding in the mountain, and that is why the moon goes away, because he cannot bear to hear her crying.

The Descent of the Corn-Queen of the Midwest

        Hades is a place I know in Ohio,
at the bottom of a long, black stair
        winding down I-76 from Pennsylvania,
        winding down the weeds
through the September damp
and that old tangled root system
of asphalt and asphodel,
        to the ash-fields,
clotted with fallen acorns
like rain puddled in fibrous pools.

        Dead hands dice onions there
on an old oak cutting board,
dead hands spackled by iron rings,
by jewels, red and dark,
        set into the skin like liver-spots,
        and all these white curls are piled before me,
old fingernails cairn-stacked.

        It is quiet in the Underworld, and every night
stews and cakes and wine appear on cedar tables,
        served by slender hands that promise
no harm, no harm
        could ever come from eating these rich and shining things.
Someone has tracked crocus petals all through the house,
a ruin of purple—
        and I cannot recall if I am allowed,
        in this place,
        to walk on it.

Don't you know these are your fruits?
Don't you know these are your flowers?

A GUIDE TO FOLKTALES IN FRAGILE DIALECTS

The pomegranates are not ripe yet,
but Ascalaphus talks shop with me
at the Farmer's Market,
        shows me Empress plums,
        papaya and mint sprigs,
        a nice Japanese pear tree of his own breed,
        heavy with colorless fruit.
The grafting process is difficult, you know,
like wedding flesh to flesh,
        and there is so much blood.

Eat.
Eat.
Don't you know these are your fruits?
Don't you know these are your flowers?

If they notice the wheat clinging to my heels,
if they are embarrassed by shreds of California
hanging from my skin like prayer flags,
they say nothing. The dead
can wait—
        by March I will glitter like them,
        my flesh a nest of stones.
Now they stir at silver pots in silence,
ladling broth over dumplings,
lips moving over incantations I cannot hear,
fingers brushing my hair as if,
        when last I was here,
they had forgotten to tell me some secret thing.

Eat.
Eat.

        They tell me the river burned here once—
the dead do not see where they are,
they think that snarl of water is the Cuyahoga,

they think that heave of grey is Erie,
          but I see, I see it,
             the Phlegethon boiling into gasoline,
braceleting the Acherusian Lake, where limbs like gasping
reach up out of the wet, clutching quarters,
Kennedy half-dollars,
pennies splashing from their blue-palmed grip.

          I see it, the smoke unfolding like a manuscript,
and fire like faces in the deep.

Don't you know these are your fruits?
Don't you know these are your flowers?

The Frog-Wife

Lean down to me,
to my green and dripping mouth—

I will tell you a secret.

Frogs keep secrets like flies:
black and sweet, under the tongue,
squelching under swamp mud,
under webbed feet,
under rotting cattails.

Lean down to me—
lean down, I cannot reach—
lean down,
down to me,
and I will lift my long red tongue.

That day—
that day when the sun
was silver in the marsh-fog—
that day I did not catch
your arrow in my mouth.

I meant to catch it—
I meant to dazzle you
with my dexterity,
with my grace. But

      the silvered sun flashed in its feathers,
      and it entered
      the loose and mottled skin below my lip
      cutting through the thin jaundice-yellow flesh—
          and if I had been singing just then,
          if it had been full as a little wet moon,

the shaft would have killed me.

Instead, it punched through my silence
like a fist through gauze,
and the roof of my mouth broke open—
blood splashed down
as through a thatch,
as if it meant to fall neatly into a tin pail,
and could not understand
why there was nothing to catch it
but my wide, quiet throat.

I drew it out of me, wrapped
in willow-whip-fingers,
and I did not cry,
for frogs cannot.
       It pulled loose
          like a lover leaving my body.

And you came just then, just then,
dragging slime-scoured boots
through salamanders' nests—
you came just then,
when I held your arrow in my little hand,
surprised at its weight,
coughing back my hanging strips of skin,
and staring,
staring
with these old black
unweeping eyes.

I swallowed my own blood,
and the silvered sun was behind you
like an icon set carefully
on a cracked and dusty mantle.
I swallowed it all,

though my ribboned throat
flapped like a drowning thing.
I swallowed—
        and held out the arrow to you,
        with a maiden's well-bred smile.

You did not see my blood's sheen
or how the feathers stuck together,
slippery and red.
        But you covered my bald green head
        when the rain came
        with the tails of your fur-trimmed coat,
and I was so warm, Ivan Tsarevitch,
so warm,
against your skin.

The thatch of your house never leaked,
and my head was never cold—
each night you lay closer to me,
and each night I smelled less and less
of eels and grasshoppers.

Each night you came nearer to me,
and I thought the three rubbery chambers
of my marsh-sodden heart would seize
like three struck drums.
        And once—oh, once!—you put your hand
        over my throat,
        and for a moment I thought you knew,
        I thought you knew.
But you moved in your sleep
and your fingers, your golden fingers,
fell away.

And I would whisper,
when the night brought you to me:

Kva, kva, Ivan Tsarevitch?
Why do you look so sad?

I think,
I think I only wanted
to hear you speak to me
like a wife.

Kva, kva, Ivan Tsarevitch?
Why do you look so sad?

Even so I wove you the shirt you wanted,
though my wet, bulging hands
bruised and bled under the needle.

Even so I baked you bread you wanted
and glazed it over with honey,
though my leaf-colored fingers
blistered on the oven.

Even so I made myself a woman,
because you wanted it, Ivan Tsarevitch,
because you wanted it.
And I wore nothing but white and silver—
       save that I could not wear those pretty shoes,
       I could not fit their arches,
       but laced up long boots
       to hide the spider-pale webbing
       still strung between my woman-toes.

I know you only wanted to keep me—
I should not have put those pearls in my hair;
I should not have caught up my waist in silk,

it was too soon, too soon—
but I only wanted to keep you.

    It is all right.
I forgave you
before you ever found that little bundle
under the stairs,
all wrapped up in tamarind leaves.

I felt it in my throat first,
that old scarred sac
that once bellowed at the moon—
I felt it there, like the arrow,
a scald, as though a bubble
had burst in a boiling pot.
    I clutched at the place
    where you first entered me,
clawed at it, and could not breathe.

You burned up my skin, Ivan Tsarevitch,
and the emerald of it,
the emerald which cost me so much,
turned black
and curled in at the edges
like a ruined book.

    It is all right.
I do not mind
that you could not wait.
I wanted you, too,
and some days
the skin weighed so heavy
my bones wept.

Happily, oh, happily
have I bled and burned for you,

Ivan Tsarevitch,
happily have I torn open
both a wide, rose-strewn breast
and a muddy cheek,
cold and small.

Because we could not wait,
you and I,
I am lying on the edge of the sky,
and my legs have long swung over.

But because of that slashed song-sac,
because of those scorch-tracks on the skin,
    I know you
are even now
listening to the tinny voices
of rabbits
and ravens
and pike flashing
in running water.
    I know you
are even now
sleeping with the fur-trimmed coat
against your unshaven face.
    I know you
are even now drawing that old arrow
from your beaten leather quiver.
    and I know
you see it—
you see it suddenly,
in a flash of sun,
showing silver through the fog,
my blood,
my first blood,
still bright and slick
along the stiff fletch of feathers.

Rampion

I was a room full of myself;
Curved walls wound round
with my own hair,
coarse and brown as homespun rope.
It smelled of nothing but me,
a dust-filthy, half-green scent
like potato sprouts dried and hung.

I remember marking out the time
on the length of my braid:
little scraps of ribbon:
red for the damp days,
green for the first of each month,
blue for the new year.
I remember shivering on a little silver footstool,
milkteeth chattering,
listening to my hair grow.

It sounded like crickets whispering.

Then: footsteps each night
when my hair was still short,
dependable as winter,
a palsied hand clutching a cup
of licorice and valerian tea.
> *Sleep liebling, sleep meine tochter.*
> *Sleep and dream of growing things,*
> *of long vines and pumpkin leaves,*
> *of radishes and raspberries,*
> *of rampion and rutabaga,*
> *of planting fingernails underneath the marjoram*
> *at the new moon.*
> *She could never have loved you so well as I.*

I slept.
My hair strangled sparrows in the eaves.

She could never feed me, was the trouble.
Witches don't have breasts, you know.
They try to hide it,
in voluptuous suits,
high, plunging collars,
so much moon-dark black silk,
but beneath it—will you believe me
if I whisper to you that
they are like angels,
nude, unmarked, smooth as marble?
My mouth found no milk in her,
though I wept and suckled at a white wall
and called her *mama, mama,*
while my cheeks sunk in.

Wise as a walnut rattle,
she opened up books printed on appleskins.
While I wailed for her body in a cradle
hollowed from a green gourd,
she rocked me with her foot on a wide porch,
grimoires open on her lap like seed catalogues,
and the sun warm on her black dress.

With a moon-crooked grin,
she gave me carrots to suck,
and parsnips, turnips,
beets like blood-smears,
squash and pea-pods, corn-ears,
peppers burning like stakes on my lips,
chicory and watercress, eggplant,
cucumber, garlic and fennel, chard,
ginger, and long green leeks.

My arms grew long and white,
root-fibrous, with pale brown lines
winding round like the scars of old rings.
My fingers were thin, long as love,
twisted up like parsnip-tips,
my face beet-bright, my eyes leafy, unfurling.
And how my hair grew and grew,
until, when I was twelve,
she simply tottered up the stairs
to water me
and spread my braids out in the sun.

What would you have been,
she whispered, saliva threading her gums,
if I had left you to her sagging breast
and cow-teat bottles?
Meat? Bone? Milk? Blood?
Can you not love me, liebling,
who nestled you in a tower—
a plant will grow only so great as its pot.
Can you not say this is better?

How many times I wrapped
my parsnip-arms around her,
closed my wispy, corkscrewed fingers
over her skinny shoulders
and pressed her old, sorrowing head
to my rampion-breast,
which was no breast at all,
but pale cabbage-leaves,
thatch upon thatch.

                                   I forgive you,
                                   I forgive you.

A ladder of tangle-roots,

my tumbling hair. What should a daughter do
when her mother
can no longer climb the stairs? I fed her
the medicines of my ribs,
the tinctures of my clavicle.
I stroked her empty chest,
and pressed my own to hers.

                    I forgive you.

Let down your hair.

                    I am so thirsty, mother,
                    why does it not
                    rain for me each evening
                    as it used to do?

She was dead by the time you came,
and I put my fingers into her mouth:
tomato-flowers burst from her teeth,
onion-stalks trickled green from her open eyes.

You saw a tower wrapped in vines,
in cornstalks like knotted ropes.
You slashed into them, searching for a door,
and I cried out three times. You heard only the sweetness
of wind singing through basil and mint,
and looked up, starving,
your teeth wet and white.

Sedna, Submerged

I.

Father, forgive me,
                    I was so hungry.
I opened my eyes—one at a time,
as each lid came free of mother
like a pair of rough pearls pulled
from a closed fist.

It was all I could do not to chew the sinews
from her thigh as I was drawn out by dry, flat hands.
It was so thick with meat and fat,
the smell of tallow and sealskin.

Her milk fell through me;
                    mother-swollen, I starved.

It began with the basket—
I only meant to suckle the furs
to soothe my breast-chafed gums,
I swear it, but the musk of their bristles,
and the salt-pelt!
                    I swallowed it all,
and a wet, black stain
spread out beneath me
stinking of shame.

It was the ice-house, then, and the caribou-bone slats
arching up towards the smoke-hole,
and the lichen (rich as crisped fishtail!),
the grated hearth, smoky and coarse—
my mouth unlatched to take it all,
quietly, quietly, so that I would not wake
mother and father, whose breath rattled.

the white floors and the clumping snow,
thick splinters of chair and bed-post.
But these too fell through my ribs,
like ice-shavings through a bone-sieve.
                        House-bloated, I starved.

Father, forgive me
                     I was so hungry.
I watched you as you slept, muscles shining
in the moon, rubbed with seal-oil,
hard and bright. I could smell the salt of your body,
and my mouth wept for you.

An arm, I thought, could not be too much
for a daughter to ask—
no father would deny it, not when his girl's
belly howled so,
a waste of tundra under her navel.

I am sorry, I am sorry,
but it was so sweet,
like blood-broth boiling.

II.

Please.

Please. Let me up.

I will not do it again. I will be a good girl.
I will make you a new arm of moss and wolfbone.

(The canoe rocked in the dark water,
and I clutched uselessly at the leather rim,
my wet, black hair streaming over the sea,
and gooseflesh rose on my skin,

ocean-sodden, shivering,
under your impassive stare.)

It is cold down here, Father.
Let me back up, let me into the boat.
I know you did not mean it,
the current was so rough,
and I must have fallen—
I must have fallen.

(I will remember this, years hence, in the dark.
The flick-flash of a stone knife—)

No, Daddy, you're hurting me—

(your pursed lips
as you sawed through skin, knuckle, marrow—)
            Oh, please, I want to go home—
            (the little splashes
as my fingers tumbled off, one by one,
into the black sea—)
            I'm sorry, I'm sorry,
I'll be good,
I'm afraid, please—
        (the thumbs last,
scrabbling at the edge of the canoe, difficult
to cut through—)
            Daddy, Daddy, I can't hold on,
help me, help—

(so white, so white in the water,
like dead things, like snow, and your face
rising away.

You did not cry at all.)

III.

I fell a long way. All around,
my fingers floated like severed tusks,
their whiteness a comfort.

But these too left me, becoming
unasked,
walrus, sea-lion, whale,
fingernails stretching into narwhal.
My own flesh swam slowly away from me,
afraid, too, of my yawning throat.

Which of us did that, Father? Which of us
should be called leviathan-god?

I watched them go.

You have rebuilt the house by now,
but I am not invited;
I am still hungry, you argue,
and mother treasures her new hearth,
the basket-pelts, her ice-throne.

Besides, my stump-hands embarrass
the new children.

The seafloor is a frozen waste,
and I starve there, wrath-blue,
under the glacier-ceiling,
my wet, black hair spreading out from me
like stones growing. It is
cold in Adlivun,
where you buried me,
and I cannot tell the souls from kelp,
the chum you spill overboard each night,

that drift down to me like thumbs,
like snow.

The Child Bride of the Lost City of Ubar

Ubar, also called Iram, established around 3000 B.C. on the Arabian Peninsula, was once the center of the frankincense trade and the wealthiest city in the world. Tradition holds that it was punished by God for its faithlessness and decadence, and the sands of the desert rose up and swallowed it whole.

I: Izdihar

Once I bathed in a basin of frankincense
once I drank a resin-tea both red and clouded
once *hojari* flowers wove through my hair:
Such was the wealth of Ubar in days long dim,
when we did not know what gold was.

Once the streets were slick and fragrant;
every alley-crack was filled with hard sap and gleaming.
My sandals used to slip on the gloss, rich as yolk,
in the summer when the sun was a long white shriek.
I used to go out into the dust-green groves;
the tree-cleavers swung me laughing between them.
Once I licked the slashed sap from the *hojari*—
it tasted bitter, like old glass.
                      like sweat, amber pooled in my navel,
as though I were a tiny cup,
filled up to brimming with the blood of Ubar.

II: Iram of the Pillars

Into the bases of seventy-two pillars
was poured *al-luban*,
the milk-sap of vivisected trees. From these heights
long fern-strands hung like wet linen, tipped in sapphire
which had puddled and run in the heat—

even our houseplants had their regalia.

                        It used to fall to the waxen curb-side,
drop by drop—
that slow gem-melt
was then our only rain.

The great market: a platform between towers,
eight-sided; shaded in red yellow-silk.
The air hung like draperies,
and no scent was there of myrrh or cinnamon—
frankincense held us all by the wrists,
and permitted no alloy.

In the great market: a cistern, bronze, bright
as a seraph's immolation.
A slow simmer of the cloud-stitched sap
bubbled all the hours of night and noon—
into this seethe of sweetness, each man dips his ladle.
                                  Such was the wealth of Ubar
when we minted coins in resin
and chewed mint leaves rubbed with palm oil.

III: Izdihar

They chose me for my hair, I think. When my mother
was as full of me as a barrel of uncrushed grapes,
she leaned over the rim of the cistern—
it burned her belly in a long red line
so well did the sun bake the metal to glowering—
to fill her diamond ladle with incense. She fell
like an onion into stew, her fast-sinking fingertips
caught by my father,
(a maker of shoes cut from emerald and porphyry),
who would not lose his wife to the boil.

A portent: she did not burn skin from bone
under the sap-liquor. They scraped it from her like honey,
and the glimmering mire that sloughed from her
made the finest perfumes of the year. But when I was born
my hair was the color of frankincense, and my eyes:
                              Such was my strangeness
that marked me among all children
beneath the pillars' blazing shade.

IV: Ubar, the Lost

We chose her for her hair.
And for the thinness of her wrists
and the promise of her hips,
which seemed to foreshadow sons,
and for the way she played in the alley-ways,
the slip-jump
of her dancing gait on sap-strung terraces.
                              We had to choose someone.
al-Raml was cast, flung high
into the shadowless sun:

The sands showed the fourth daughter conjunct.
Prophets always did a brisk business here—
they wept and refused their ladles,
keened and preached that we should not have worshipped
the pillar-gods with their stone breasts, their resin-altars,
should not cast *al-Raml*, should not do this,
should not do that.
                              But the truth is:
the desert is always thirsty.
It needs no reason to drink.

The sand-augur shouted down the howl of holies:
the dunes do not thirst but lust. Give them
a daughter of Ubar and they will quiet, they will recede,

they will retire to a dusty wedding-bed curtained
with saltbush and mouse-bones.
                              Her maidenhead
will feed dwarf-acacias
and pale yellow spiders.

V: Izdihar

Even among the seventy-two pillars whose roofs
bruise the stars' bellies, I had never known anything
so fine as the black veils of my wedding dress.
The scent of the veils against my nose was of skin
and emerald dust, and frankincense, always frankincense,
that slow rosy sigh.

I walked to the edge of the sand
where the palm fronds wither,
and behind me walked Ubar,
cymbals clanging, throats ululating—
trumpets announced my virginity
to the crawling gray scrub.
A red ribbon was laid over my wrist,
and over a rise of rough sand—
                              I swore to obey it, and serve it,
and bear it children
with yellow eyes running over like hourglasses.

In the desert, the nights are colder than you expect:
The resin hardens. The cistern cools. I was afraid—
the moon was so dry and empty,
a bone bowl filling up with sky.
I was knotted to a stake deep-driven,
spangled with sapphire-rain—
they had known better than to let me choose.
Long hours ground against me. The wind came up
through the white grasses.

                              A skinny, dry-whiskered mouse
                              darted near—
in the marrow-sucked moonlight,
he began to nibble my toes.

VI. Rub' al-Khali: The Empty Quarter

Perhaps it did not love her. She was so strange, after all.
The desert did not push open her untried legs
and forget us in the sweetness of her mouth.
                              It did not want her.
Perhaps a black-haired girl
would have satisfied it.

The pillars fell onto the sand softer than memory.
Even we did not hear them go—until all the eyes of Iram
were drowned in a shower of gold.

The earth was wet for years afterward, wet and glittering
and stinking of incense,
so that even the fleas would not come near.
The cistern soaked the earth for miles,
though the ash-sand covered the market like a page.
                    Such was the death of Ubar
when the desert unhinged its jaw,
when the desert did not want her.

There are no bones here, not even hers. We sank so far
we tasted water—
water at the root of all this rainless waste.
But it is not deep enough, never deep enough
to find silence.
We still hear it, we still hear it and there are no palms left
to press against desiccated ears,
we hear and hear and cannot stop:
                              Such are the wails

of Izdihar the Dune-Wed,
who yet pleads to come home.

Tale Type -17:
The Courtship of Heaven and Earth

Courtship rituals among the inhabitants of the long, rich banks of the ———— River are complex and highly stylized, informed by a particular story told by the prospective bride to the prospective husband. His responses to her variant determine his worth as a spouse. Young women are encouraged to change any details they wish so as to trip up their suitors. The following version was told to an extremely discomfited Japanese undergraduate at the turn of the century. He was eventually able, through somewhat indelicate means, to collect over three hundred variations on this theme.

Once Lady Almond wished to marry, and journeyed to the land of King Tobacco to do so. The distance between her country and his was very great, and along the way she met the sun, who was very handsome, strolling with a cane in his hand and a hat on his head. "I am green and young and in need of marriage," Lady Almond said brightly. The sun blushed red. "I have never been asked for my hand," he said, "and so I am bashful and shy." But Lady Almond took his hand, though he burned her skin brown as a nut, and they were happy together.

But time passed, and Lady Almond grew weary of the sun's constant heat. She resumed her journey towards the land of King Tobacco. But the distance was still very great from the house of the sun, and along the way she met the moon, who was very solemn, walking through a meadow with a long cloak sweeping the grass. "I am brown and hale and in need of marriage," Lady Almond said boldly. The moon grew pale. "No one has ever thought to ask for my hand," he said, "and so I am innocent and anxious." But Lady Almond took his hand, though he froze her white as bark, and they were happy together.

But time passed, and Lady Almond grew weary of the moon's unchanging cold. She resumed her journey towards the land of King Tobacco. But the distance was still very great from the village of the moon, and along the way she met the evening star, who was very merry, dancing along the river with a flower in his teeth. "I am white and wry and in need of marriage," Lady Almond said. The star shone brightly. "My hand has gone unasked for all these years," he said, "and so I am eager and willing." Lady Almond took his hand, though he was so bright that he shrunk her to the size of a seed, and they were happy together.

But time passed, and Lady Almond grew weary of the star's constant light. She resumed her journey towards the land of King Tobacco, which was not now very far from the hut of the star. The castle of King Tobacco was tall and brown and warm, and Lady Almond entered and found the King waiting for her on his throne of leaves. "I am old, and dry, and shrunken," she said, "and I have had my fill of marriage." King Tobacco, whose face was very dark, almost skeletal, smiled. "Rest here with me, then," he said, and became smoke, thick and fragrant, which lifted Lady Almond, who was by then so small and light that she was no more than a seed husk, out of the castle and into the night, where her former husbands gathered to bid her farewell.

Skadi in the Forest of Legs

I.

I came to the scrim of heaven with Idun's apples
strung through my hair like clay beads.
I came to the scrim of heaven with my father's acrid wings
stinking of roasted bones.
I came to the scrim of heaven with a single red fruit
bound into my hoary jaws like a gag.

I came to the ash-pale walls of Hrimthurs the rime-giant
on silver snowshoes lashed with pine.
I came to the bronze-bolted door of Gladsheim
with my chest girded in ice.
I came to the wasted plain of Ida
and snapped the red fruit to its seedy core.

My hands were full of death and they paid me
with red-bearded laughter—
I held out my father's denuded corpse,
embalmed in a smear of apple meat
no more beautiful or fell
than a rooster plucked for feasting.

I asked for death-payment.
I asked for weregild bright and cold.
I asked for grief and long laments.
I asked for black veils and mead-songs.

But they gamboled like village fools,
heads all motley velvet and jangling bells.
They leapt around me like mummers,
leering with pumpkin-faces and lantern-eyes.
They made my father's dead limbs to dance
with shambling steps.

I cared nothing for their sport, and I expected
nothing of their gold.
I came to take from them—it is the right
of winter to take, to make bereft, to steal away
in the night's freeze. And so, when the horse-haired one
tied himself to a goat, and all looked to me
to see me laugh like birches shaking,
I let my lips curl back
into something like a smile.
I let my orphaned throat
croak and tear,
and the sound was not unlike mirth.

These were the funeral rites of Thjazi Storm-Boar:
a blonde drunkard knotting his testicles to a goat's tail.

II.

Instead of gold they piled up gods
like logs on a steam-morned riverside.
Instead of gold they laid out husbands
one after the other, like a hundred shackles
shaped to my own wrists.
Instead of gold, they showed me men,
nothing but men, hairy and dull as wattle.

Oh, they will tell you I was a silly girl—
vain as swans, eyes full of pig-lust.
They will tell you I was enthralled of
that line of stinking feet, the yellow nails
and matted hair, the calf-muscles like sacks
of beef, thighs reddened with the wind I bellow,
the winter I carry with me
like a son gnawing at my breast.
They will tell you my eyes were full

of those mange-ridden shepherds
scratching at their bellies.

It is true that there was one pair of feet
more beautiful than all the rest—
if beauty can be said to lie
in the brine-crusted ankles
of a fisherman dragging
his nets and cages behind him.

Surely, surely one of those cages
was the right size for me.

I put my white hand on the sand-scoured calf,
the calf which came from dunes blown with wildflowers
and barnacles warm and wet on ship-shanks—
frost crept over the coarse black hairs.
Icicles formed on the knobbled toes.
A thin drift of snow sifted onto the skin.

They cackled like a cat-chorus, clapping each other
about the shoulders, laughing again, again,
through their golden beards and décolletage—
certain I meant to chose their prettiest boy,
certain I meant to mount the square-jawed bowman
with the shadow of mistletoe greening his breast.

How unfortunate, they clucked, that the stupid milkmaid
fell in love with the whale-ribbed sea god instead!
Women are such greedy, frivolous little mice,
are they not?

I hissed like snowshoes sluicing through the tundra,
and in the daisy-spring of Asgard
I froze the beard of the sea-rat.

III.

I came to the scrim of heaven with Idun's apples
strung through my hair like clay beads.
I came to the scrim of heaven with my father's acrid wings
stinking of roasted bones.
I came to the scrim of heaven with a single red fruit
bound into my hoary jaws like a gag.

I am the berry flash-frozen in December—
I am the reindeer's tracks.
I am the storm-god's daughter—
I am the death of all apples.

With a breastplate of snow-cased branches
I stole the warm ocean-wind,
the pleasant waters salt and shallow,
the summer tidepools red and green.
I took the shipwright with his cloak of oars,
I took the brawling, bright-haired boy
who was loved well.

I set foxes on his cages and unloosed
a slough of flashing fish from his oily nets.
In the crags of Thrymheim I closed him up—
silvered those fat calves in ice.
My chaste wedding kiss
shriveled his tongue black and gangrene—
and it was then,
for the first time,
that his blue-thumbed body seemed beautiful,
and I laughed in the star-clotted mist,
in my orphaned throat.

Before his great glass stalactite
I lay my father's acrid wings,

a sacrifice still smoking.
Poor, broken things:

all those ashen feathers,
drifting in the sea-tinged air
like snowflakes.

The Gardener and the Grave-Keeper

He stood in her doorway like a planted bramble;
                she stood aside,
                and drew away—
but his voice grazed her cheek sun-sallow,
and his whisper
pulled at her gauzy sleeve:

"Under your white wrist I open my jaw
under your cold chin I split my teeth
under you, O colorless , O maid,
I hinge and splay my tongue—
and there is a rose there,
                a red rose, aye, and fair.

You could pluck this thing from me,
                aye, this red, red thing,
and I would be your own brown-bellied boy;
I would sew you up a dress of lilies,
a thread of soft stems
(dandelion and daisy, by measure mine)
glinting green in the seam
                for nothing which is not root-pure
                should brush the landscape of your skin.

And I would draw a coat of camellia
over your shoulders, patched with ivy and vine.
I would pull gloves of marigold over your hands,
and I would cinch your waist with a skirt of salad-greens,
sleek your calves with wide, grassy stalks.
And I would cap your hair—O lightless hair!—with gilly-flower,
pin primrose to your breast as pearl.

You could pluck this thing from me,
                aye, this red, red thing,

let it stain your pristine fingers—
for I would plant this thing in you,
and erase your flesh with flowers,
vanish you in flora until your own sweet mouth
floods itself with petals,
petals red and fair.

I would cover you in boughs
(if you would not say me nay)
until your belly lay beneath me
framed in sap and green—
then—O then!—I would crack your flesh door-open,
cross you like a threshold,
to find beneath your reedy navel
the hidden sun, gold and pale,
a burning cuff around your spine.

And on this disc, this red, red disc,
I would place my rose,
tongue to bone, tongue to bone.

Say you'll take my rose from me,
say you'll let the sun
dribble out between your hipbones—
I will crown you high in summer sweet,
and feed you from my own bright lips
like the blue-beaked hoopoe
succors her young."

But the white-cheeked maid drew back from him,
and her breath was chill on his chin:

"I will not take that thing from you,
        nay, not that red, red thing—
it would burn me so.

You would melt me all away
and be my sop-soaked boy,
all drenched in my ruin,
all silver with my ruin—
why would you hold such a thing out to me,
bloody and scalding, bloody and bright?

I will not take it, I will not take it—

but you could take this cold from me,
            aye, this pale, pale thing,
and be my own brack-barren boy.

And I could sew you up a smock of snow,
a crown of broken branches;
I could sleek your calves in ice and stone,
I could cap your hair—O downy hair!—in whipping wind,
clap rain to your breast as iron.

I could cover you in sleet
(if you would not say me nay)
until your broad back lay beneath me
framed in yew and howl—
then—O then!—I would crack your skin grave-open
climb you like a stair
and find beneath your hail-strewn bones
the hidden moon, half in shadow,
a breathing ring around your spine.

And on this sickle, this pale, pale scythe,
I would place my freezing kiss,
tongue to bone, tongue to bone."

She stood in her doorway like a twisted ice-slough;
          he stood aside,
          and bolted away

though her voice grazed his cheek moon-fallow,
and her whisper
snagged his coarse-sewn sleeve.

Tale Type 10,441:
The Woman Who Married the Land

In the insular cultures of the greenest plains, there is a tale which no one is allowed to tell, but which everyone knows. A professor of Canadian folklore spent seven years in an attempt to determine sources or methods of transmission. She met with no success, whether because the plainswomen are truculent with outsiders or because they simply absorb the story in a kind of pre-cognitive state of grace she found it impossible to guess.

There was once a woman so clever that the sun burned terribly bright on the day she was born, having at last found someone with whom it could share some comradely feeling. The girl was so clever that everyone thought her beautiful. In time she married a man who could do all manner of interesting things with his hands and his head, and he took her to the greenest fields of the green plains, and there built a house with several windows and at least two doors. But the clever woman found that once she was inside the house it grew more and more difficult for her to get out; more and more of the windows and doors were locked from the outside, and as she bore her clever husband children, she became more and more still, until she could not move at all. Yet still her husband kissed her at the end of the day, and smiled, and saw nothing the matter, and still her children played children's games at her immobile feet. The clever woman felt her cleverness becoming still within her, too, and was afraid. But her husband told her she was more beautiful than ever, and lovingly brought her dinners to the hallway where she was rooted.

In time the other families of the green plains came to see the woman, who was no longer very clever at all, staring dumbly from her hall to the locked door. But it was only the husbands and sons who came, and the woman was not so insensate that she did not notice it. Finally, when her oldest child went away to school, the woman's feet broke through the floor of her house of many windows, and sank into the rich soil of the plains. There her toes left aside their stillness and grew like fleshy roots, burrowing through the dirt with blind abandon, growing, worm-like, curious. One evening, when her husband was brushing her hair in the great hall, her toes touched something warm: the toes of another woman, rooted in another house, rooted in the green plains. The clever woman understood why only husbands and sons had visited her, and her toes searched out the other plainswomen, motionless in their houses, rooted in hall and bath and bed, and while her long hair was combed and set by a happy man, she wept.

The Queen of Hearts

      "I am Lost,"
said the Queen of Hearts
to the Queen of Spades,

      "and my rouge has spoilt in its pot.
The scarlet is quite ruined—
and it's just the season for reds, you know."

      "I do not,"
replied the Queen of Spades,
"for I have always found black
to suit perfectly.

      My collar is black,
      and my buttons,
      and my petticoats
      and my slippers.

      At any rate, you use far too much of that rot.
Paleness is next to purity—
or haven't you read the latest novels?"

      "It was the King of Clubs who did it,
of course. His doublet is terrifically gauche—
last year's shade of jet, don't you think?
And the hose are not to be borne."

      "I'm quite sure I haven't the first idea
what sputters out of your painted mouth these days,"
      sniffed the Queen of Spades,
      her black eyes hard a-glitter.

      "He made me Lost," whispered the Queen,
and red was the color of her voice. "Behind the roses,

Tuesday last. He took off his gloves—
    they sloughed like skin!—
and the hands beneath were crow's claws,
less yellow than rooster; not so grey as dove."

    The Queen of Spades snapped her lacy fan
quick as whisking eggs. "Darling, you've been in the heat
far too long. Come under the canopy,
you know the sun
works miseries on the complexion."

    "You know perfectly well
my cheek is famed in five counties.
No, I'm afraid
it was no dream, no dream at all."
    The Queen of Hearts cradled her voice in a whisper.
    "The roses were so red, you know.

    His curls had the color of inkspill,
and his eyes no iris at all—
My breath was in a swoon,
my tongue
and my voice,
    when those black spurs brushed my throat.
    And, my dear, I can hardly speak it,
I hesitate to confess—though our sorority is sacrosanct—"

    The Queen of Spades said nothing,
but inclined her head in the sun.

    "He smiled at me, a courtly smile, fit for any duchess,
while they wormed and wheedled, wriggled and wove
into my skin,
and my bone.

    A Queen possesses tears, of course,

beyond the grief of other women.
These crystal drops
branded my cheeks
    —famed though they be—
and seeped into the wound that even then widened
about the thickness of his crow's foot
that ground and scraped within.

    O sister mine, I could feel it so, like a lizard
scrabbling in the sand for beetles.

    And indeed, how like a scarab it was
when he drew it from me;
carnelian, garnet,
that stony red bullet in his clutch:

    a Heart, tiny as a bead strung on silk,
unbeating, wet. He smiled
his ducal smile,
and popped it between his supple lips,
with a wink and a doff of his cap,
just as if it were penny candy.

    And ever since,
I have been Lost; my skin cannot hold
its color.

But the roses, you know,
the roses are still so red."

    The Queen of Spades knitted her brow—
as fine a brow as ever sat
on a lady of rank in the realm—
and covered her face with her fan.
    "You ought not to have tattled,"
said she,

"though the story itself was well-told.
Black must side with Black, you know,
and shun the Red for knaves."

    At this the dark Queen parted her lips
and extended her delicate tongue:
it sat in the crease of the pink,
like a signet nestled in its box,

    a Heart, tiny as a bead strung on silk,
unbeating, wet.

    She lapped it back with relish and glad,
and red was the color of her cheek.

    "Your slippers, " said the Spade, "do not quite match
your train. Tragic, of course,
but one must make allowances for breeding."
    The Heart slumped suddenly
in her blood-bright palanquin.
    "Now come into the parlor, there's a girl,
you've tired yourself with prattling."

    The Black Queen led the Red
from the garden,
with eight bald men to bear the pall,
    for the sun had knelt in the sky.

And beneath that spotless glove,
black as the swans of Aethiop,
    her crow-crook sat warm, flat
    on her sister's scarlet knee.

Pasiphae's Machine

I only needed the bull to set it going:
a bone key turning,
a hide bolt locking
into place.

I went to his house like a spice-buyer,
clutching my elbows. Away from my husband
for the first time since he fished me
thrashing from the sea
with a line of spider-silk
and a terra-cotta hook (my mother
had no better: the sun shone on her waves
and she found herself a blue ball,
full of queens.) I ran my hands
over mason jars and silver gears,
tin-and-ivory wings with harnesses of linen,
floor-tiles, serpent-jaws,
pipes and joinings
like white arms clutched in jeweled fists.

He was covered in iron filings and red dust,
his back turtle-hunched. He did not
even look at me,
but continued to tap
at a glass nail
with a diamond hammer.

You will need to be fitted,
like a dress to a waist.

Daedalus, no stranger to perversion,
pushed his spectacles
up the bridge of his nose.

My arm looks so small
in the bronze vise—the lynch-pin
slides through the delicate
fish-pale bones
of my wrist.

Every month
he widens the punctures.
I can hold six bolts in me, now,
crossed like rafters
through my breasts.

He lays a copper spine to my back,
knobbled with wire.

He fixes discs to my knees,
bowl-curved and singing.

He closes up my head
in a sphere of horned gold—
I did not want eye-sockets;
he smoothed them over
with lead, soft as wet sand.

Every month
he grinds the saw-toothed moon
along my shoulder blades,
and shunts another bolt
though my ankle,
my navel,
my mouth.

I gleam, rivet to spike
to bone:

latitudes hinged by stars.

I only needed the bull to set it going:
a battery of horn and gristle,
a switch of tail and hoof.

He left me on the dancing-floor,
whorled in super-conducting coils,
plated in mis-matched metals
which did not look unlike
a heifer's patched skin.

I waited. The birds kept clear.

Steam fogged the tin withers,
in the close, in the dark,
in the cloud of breath,
     the bull closed the circuit,
and the bolts ground into motion,
moving in me like light,
a skeleton of glittering pistons
clattered into place—
bull-belly lifting up,
pins jingling, high and sweet,
and oh! The slick shove of them,
the sigh of bronze against bronze,
and I did not need the bull
but I will take it:
twins to batter this dusty island:
a bull-child and his favorite toy.

They will lie so sweetly,
thumb curved into wall,
nub-horns and a tiny, soft tail

within an infant labyrinth
of bronze and skin and silver,
angled and folded,
like the legs of their mother
finally buckling
under so much weight.

The Inkmaker's Wife

They lie over every square of grass-strewn floor,
like pans set out to catch the rain
from a poorly-thatched roof.
China pots with blue rims, milk pitchers, gravy-boats,
silver tureens and fingerbowls, coffee-cups, mason jars,
saucepans and green-necked wine bottles,
painted kettles, even
my grandmother's gold-speckled urn,
her ashes having long been packed into a tea-box
and tucked away in a drawer—
he promised to replace them,
as soon as there was room enough—
all brimming with ink like smoke
drifting in under the door,
the black of it hypnotic, the color
of dead pupils.

In wire baskets, he brings the week's cuttlefish
squirming wetly, their skin frantic,
flushing the pattern of the mesh,
trying to disappear—but their soft faces
flutter under the wooden hammer, and in despair,
in death-convulse, sepia slavers from their flesh
into a clay bowl. He cuts the little sac away
with my cheese-knife, and the meat
will boil for stew.

Gall-nuts float in a jar which was once full
of flaxseed oil, their metallic stink like burned bread,
scraped iron drifts in the clear water of the washbasin.

Near the door, a silver bowl, scrubbed with sand,
is gorged with a perfect red he has tended
all winter—the shade of cranberries

and hymeneal ruin. It looks sacred,
a lustral font, and I have longed to anoint
my body there. *Et spiritus sancti, et spiritus,*
et spiritus,
et spiritus sancti.

When he puts his hands to my waist, in the midst
of all this captured rain, he leaves streaks of black,
of brown, of green and blue.
His fingernails are glutted with it,
his hair stiff with dyes. I am marked like a
tigress, striped, savaged. Slashes of squid-brume
criss-cross my throat like migrations,
and my navel catches its share of sweat-pigment
beading on his brow. I am
the leaves of a book; my bones join the spine of
a pre-history, glyphs of mammoth
and plesiosaur, of spermatozoa and sun-worship.

He groans wordlessly; his hands smell of walnut-leech.

Naked, I am written—but the ink is not his,
nor the marrow-alphabet. The cuttlefish trace
their glottals onto the cave-walls of my ribs,
bubbling out of his pores, his teeth, his lips.
I lie eager beneath their ululating mouths,
and he does not guess at our salt-blotted cuneiform.

Over the Edda of my morning-skin I fasten
a yellow cotton dress, a leather belt, a clean apron.
The bowl of scarlet ink receives the light,
slicing through two panes of window-glass,
like a flayed heart.

Helen in the Underworld

It was in Egypt. I found them in Egypt:
        little oily seeds.
        iridescent, almost,
like hummingbird pupils.

There was sand in your eyebrows
when you gave them to me,
sand in the creases of apothecary-palms.
Your eyes were full of mercury and gypsum,
overflowing with bryony and hellebore.
        I thought the venom-glut meant
        you were to be trusted.
You promised to make of me
        a cloud-Helen,
        a creature of vapor and moonlight.
You promised that roses would detonate in my brain,
that my heart would crack
and its ventricles would overflow
with olives and goatsblood.

You promised that oblivion
would strangle me with ringed hands.

You promised me I would remember nothing.

I took it back to my husband,
mashed the seeds with a pestle of bone.
        The sludge was so black,
        like the innards of butterflies.

It was easy to fold it into honeyed dough,
easy to smile and smile
while I crawled about his errands
on my knees, on my hands,

still boat-shackled
> as though it all happened yesterday
> and we two still sea-tossed—

no more than I deserved, he sneered.

Easy to lie on my pillows
while he gobbled up the sweets,
crumbs catching in the sheep-wool of his barrel-chest,
licking the sugar-seeds off of his beard
with a slavering tongue.

The taste of them, smeared into Stygian icing,
> was of mouse-spleens
> and burnt apples soaked in wine.

I pressed it to the roof of my mouth with my tongue.

I waited for the darkness,
I waited for the wind-torn towers
to melt in me and dribble
out of my mouth like scorched fruit.

He crawled to me on his knees,
pawing my thighs, growling that I owed him,
> I owed him,
> I owed him,

and if I had whored my swan-born body
to the leopard-slaying prince,
there was nothing I could refuse.

My jaw shattered in his fist,
my beak-golden hair tore from my scalp.
He dragged my ship-launching face
down into the depths of his beard,
> and I was not a cloud,
> I was not vapor,

I was meat and bile and his lips
were stealing my breath
and the city flamed behind me,
I could feel the heat of it still.

He broke the kitchen table when he collapsed,
insensate honey drooling from his mouth.
Blood bloomed in me,
a secret door, flesh-fluttering,
              and I fell into it,
              I fell so far,
eager for your promised ease,
eager to forget the smell of Creusa burning,
her hair sizzling into baldness,
her fingernails boiling—
I wanted to forget that spattering perfume,
forget the boy-prince and his zealous kisses,
forget her endless keening,
like a heifer slaughtered for my hecatomb.

You promised me. Sand-browed apothecary,
with your cabinet of poisons.
You promised the shades
would stop crowding me,
would stop worming their mouths into me
to warm themselves in my blood—
              but they were there,
              waiting at the bottom
of the well of my womb,
and I fell into their arms,
whimpering, begging nonsense vowels.

They opened my belly as though unfolding a blanket
over an amputee on that lonely, mussel-strewn beach—
and pulled out their dresses left on the altars—
blue and violet and green,

spangled and ivory-buttoned,
veils and furs and ribbons.

They pulled from me the hollow horse,
the sleek black ships;
they pulled from me the eggs of my birth,
the ash-spear cock of Ajax,
        and fire,
           endless buckets of fire,
passed from ghost to ghost like well-water.

They dragged Ilium from my body entire,
towers and gates and plumed helmets,
and I whispered that I was a bird, a cloud,
I had nothing but wings and air to my name,
and they could not accuse me
as though I were a woman.

But they would not listen,
they would not see the feathers I showed them,
they would not see my ruined cradle-egg.
They dug into me over and over
and pulled out their own faces,
coins blazing in their eyes.

I clutched at my belly, my swan-belly,
my vapor-belly:
it threw back the black paste onto my husband's feet.
        You lied, You lied,
           with sand in your mouth, you lied to me.
The cloud-Troy
still floats in me like a cancer,
sending its flames into the slough of asphodels
that line the curve of my skull.

It is still there, still there,

so pale, and so bright,
and I will take the mercury next,
if you will sell it to me,
and the gypsum, and the bryony,
and the hellebore,
> I have enough, more than enough
> to pay for these.
Put your quicksilver under my tongue.
> I do not mind the taste.
Make me not-Helen. Tell me
I have been here, in Egypt all along,
and I did not hear Cassandra's wrist break
on the altar steps.

Tale Type 5513A-Z: Blood Tales

Among a certain people who inhabit a network of barren deserts amid fertile lands, not unlike those who carefully inhabit only the isles of an archipelago and never the sea, there are quite simply no tales which do not involve blood. Blood is a common motif in most cultures, but for this particular tribe, no narrative structure can be conceived of which does not center around it, examine it, and rely on it utterly. A western anthropologist once tried to tell one of the elders the story of Cinderella, only to find her fixated solely upon the severed heel and toe. Upon attempting to explicate Hansel and Gretel, he found that she could not understand it at all, asked numerous questions as to the demise of the witch, and, unsatisfied, had forgotten it entirely by morning, but excitedly told her daughters of the sisters who severed their feet.

There can be no tale without blood. No oldest son can leave the tribe to seek out a great treasure in treacherous lands but that he meets a gnome who offers him the blood tea in a skull-cup, no middle son can stumble into the night past the safety of the fire-circle without coming upon a bent old man who offers him a choice of bowls, one of broth, one of water, and one of blood. No youngest child can go to war without a loyal horse whose skin splits for him at the close of every day so that he might drink her blood, becoming more and more horse and his steed less and less so, until rider and ridden are reversed. No daughter may be kidnapped away by foreigners that she will not cut open her fingertips to leave a trail for her sisters to follow, no maiden may be married against her will that she is not anointed in cockerel blood and wed with scarlet face, scarlet hands.

"A tale has blood like a body," said the elder, "and if it does not, it cannot live, no more than I."

Glass, Blood, and Ash

I.

Please, silk-sister, do this thing for me.

I do not want to sit on that broad-backed horse,
or smell his skin, grassy and hot as boiled husks,
inside a shirt ropy with gold tassels and primogeniture.

I never wanted it. I just
wanted to look like you
for one night. It should be you
hoisted up like a sack of wheat—
I stole your ruby comb,
your garnet pendant.
It must have been
your jewels he loved.

You will like it—they will put emeralds in your hair
and a thin gold crown on your head.
They will rub your skin down to supple
like a favorite tiger, soon to be
a favorite carpet.
Your spine is fit to queen-posture, not mine.

It is only a little shoe, only a little lie.
It was made from a mirror whose glass
was ground in another tale.
Look into it. It surely sings
that you are the fairer.

The doves, their claws still dusty with kitchen-ash
brought me a knife hammered out of a diamond.

It is so thin

that a breath will shatter it,
but so sharp
that the flesh it cleaves
does not even know
it has been cut.

Give me your heel.
I am the kind one, remember?
I would not hurt you.

Please, we are sisters;
out of the same striped pelt
did our father scissor our hearts.
Do this thing for me
your sister is afraid of the man
who loves her so much
he cannot remember her face.

Hold your breath—
I shall hold mine.

II.

The ash that crossed my forehead
was finer than the ash that greyed my feet—
soft as a kiss.

I wanted to dance. I wanted to be warm.
I wanted to eat. I wanted anything
but the furnace-grating cutting its
familiar welt-mark
into my back.

With my forehead exalted I went into the wood,
calling out to a dead mother
like a saint with her eyes on a plate.

But she did not come—
a nightingale instead hopped towards me
baring her little brown breast.

I am the song of your beauty, it chirped.

Like a hoopoe, she bent her head
and bit her own heart
in two. Out of her thin chest
spilled a gown red and gleaming,
bright as blisters.

It was this I wore under the palace arches,
this which cuffed my wrists,
cupped my breasts,
pinched my waist.

I walked into his arms bathed
in the blood of a nightingale,
and when we parted
he was drenched in scarlet.

III.

Please, silver-sister, do this thing for me.

I do not want to wear that dress again.
I do not want to kiss him, I do not want
to know what a prince tastes like. I do not want
to hear the castle doors shut behind me.

I never wanted it. I only wanted
to stand in that torchlight for a second
and feel as you must always feel.
It should be you hoisted up
with his saddlebags—

I stole your coral ring
and your attar of roses.
It must have been
your scent he loved.

You will like it—they will put pearls on your fingers
and a thin ivory crown on your head.
They will hang you up in a hall
and everyone will look at you,
everyone will remark how beautiful you are.
Your spine is fitted to that golden hook, not mine.

It is only a little shoe, only a little lie.
It was made from a coffin whose glass
was ground in another tale.
Look into it. It surely promises peace.

The arch is full of her blood, yes,
but that pours out as easily as soup from a ladle.

The doves, their claws still dusty with kitchen-ash,
brought me a knife hammered out of a diamond.

It is so thin
that a whisper will shatter it,
but so sharp
that the flesh it cleaves
believes itself whole.

Give me your toe.
I am the gentle one, remember?
I would not hurt you.

Please, we are sisters;
out of the same white wood
did our father hew our hearts.

Do this thing for me
your sister is afraid of the man
who loves her so much
he cannot tell her from any other.

Be silent—
so shall I.

IV.

Is there not another daughter in this house?

My hand is cold and heavy in his. The shoe
is full as a spoon, their blood
bright as blisters. My foot
glides noiseless in
on that slick scarlet track.

He tastes of dead gold.

My skin is tiger-supple,
there are emeralds in my hair,
pearls on my fingers
a thin ivory crown on my head.
I am loved; I am polished.

From my hook in the hall,
I can see the gardens.

Inhumed, Her Star-Staked Body Bloodless Lies

I: Orsolya in the Sun, Standing on One Foot

Locust-trees spit grey-spined shadows at her leg;
leaf-saliva drips into the hollow behind her knee.
Black hair, rough and bristling,
flagellates her bent and naked back.

There is stiff brown bread and milk
in a bowl by the mirror.
There is frost at the window-seam.
Snow hunkers blue-toothed
behind the bright slats of sunlight
that slash the room into shards.
Outside, a hawk lands in a shorn field,
stabs the frozen ground for mice.

She balances her foot against a little stool,
the inside of her thigh shows dull and pale:
book-open, wheat-fed, butter-soft.

I will keep very quiet, she thinks,
it will hurt, but I will stay quiet as a house.

There are five-petaled blue buds
embroidered on her curtains,
though she has never been sure
if they were meant to be violets or lettuce-flowers.
Her little rug is green with black yarn-flecks;
she used to pretend they were ants in the grass,
she chased them with her fingers.

The room is very quiet, but she has heard—
who has not heard?—the wind out of Budapest

is full of iron and oil. By the green banks of the Volga,
there is snow freezing over
in the hollows of her brothers' ears.
She has heard buckled boots
flattening wheat not far off,
not far, now. There are not even any locks
on her house.

She is a good girl. She has decided.
She has been around their dun-flanked cows
enough to know where best to open a vein.

Ludovic, she thinks, *you promised me*
a maidenhead of beef-blood
dribbled over white linen. We laughed about it,
how we would steal the heifer's heart
and mark the bed as though, after you,
I remembered what a hymen was.

Her wrists are so thin the light
comes through them like glass.
The hawk has found a brindled buck-mouse.
A long, curly slab of hair
sloughs over her shoulder,
the light between the locust-branches
ladders down from her scalp.

Quiet as a house.

She cuts open her thigh like a hen's neck.

II: Orsolya by Moonlight, Recumbent

Inhumed, her star-staked body bloodless lies,
breathes frozen dirt, chews ice-riddled loam.
Her eyes are squeezed shut as an infant cat's,

unused to light, suckling at the root-systems
of a ragged, bark-bare poplar
and an slumped, whip-limbed peach tree.
There is wind—
dry, moon-striped.

Her palms itch—locust-switches pin her asplay.
Arms point like clock-hands,
legs tied open, obscene, clay-spackled. A sparrow
skeleton nestles against the cold, clotted wound,
its hollow eyes receive flakes of dried blood
drifting through its lidless bone like wood-ash.

It is no trouble to pull herself off of the burly stakes—
she doesn't even feel her palms tear.
Blind as a grandmother, she eats her way up
through leaves and old peach-meat and frost-rigid mud.
Her stomach shows through first:
the moon draws up its own image from the earth.

Orsolya stands at the crossroads,
shivering, naked, trying to hide
her breasts with mire-smeared arms.

Gooseflesh prickles through the melting reek
that clings to her belly, shoulders, throat.
Her hair is slick with frog-skin and worm-trails;
her teeth chatter like a child caught in snow.

She turns north, south. She can smell
the flattened wheat, now burning.
She peers through the wind and moon
and long ice-dusted roads.
That way is, perhaps, the Lackzó chicken farm,
and this way, maybe,
is the gabled Szabó house

with its four daughters endlessly embroidering—
but she cannot be sure,
she cannot be sure.

Papa! I'm lost!

She calls out;
the poplar clatters hesitantly.

I'm ready to come home now! It's cold out here!

The peach tree spits
fat, wrinkled seeds after her.

*Papa! I'll catch my death of cold! Come get me,
put a red wool blanket around my shoulders.
Tell me it's going to be alright, that my brothers
are coming home safe.*

*Papa, I'm so hungry. Just call out my name—
I can follow your voice.*

The sparrow skull gapes,
its little teeth full of dirt.

Her peeled-egg eyes raw and new, she stumbles,
arms groping the shadows for purchase.
Down the west road she can smell cows:
warm, dun-gold flanks
soft, wet, snorting noses,
and she can hear a heifer's heart beating,
huge and dark as a fist,
and boots
crushing snow underfoot.

How Comes This Blood Upon the Key?

With two blue hands like slaps of freezing
you shut me up into this house. Up:
the walls. Up:
the gables. Up:
doors upon doors.
Mortar-seams boiled bright
along the drywall, bright
as bride-price.

You wrote my name on a scrap of vellum,
folded it into our wedding sheet
with its shy fall of scarlet,
tied them together with a scrap of your beard,
blue as ribbons, blue as drowning,
and shut it up into a box of gold and chrysolite.

And this you put behind a little cedar door,
and this you locked with a little golden key.

The walls clapped closed;
I forgot my name. I knew only
the scrape of your chest against mine,
the scour of your storm-strung beard,
and the press of the dove-bare rafters on my shoulders.

With two blue hands like welts of seeming,
you shut me up into this house,
into this body which is called wife,
and left me.
You left me alone,
and the light through the windows
was plague-pale, gaunt.

Your only words to me in years:

Do not touch the little golden key.
Do not open the little cedar door.

I did not, as some gold-laced women will,
go into the wood looking for this house,
any house,
any place to be closed up
away from wolves. I did not look
for a house to become my limbs,
for cast iron pans to become my joints,
for doors and keys to become
the stuff of my blood,
for a bed to become my face.

You came dragging this house behind you,
and the moon was cradled in your beard.
You fit it to me, tight as a belt,
and left me gasping
while you walked the world
in boots of quicksilver
and militant mule-skin.

Do not touch the little golden key.
Do not open the little cedar door.

I was looking
for my name.

Yes, I meant to leave you.

It did not seem right,
that in my own body,
there was a place I could not look.

I went through the wine cellar,

the broom closet,
the larder with its dusty jars
of peach jam and old flour.
It was there, nestled into the earth,
like a mouth slapped shut.

The key slid in as easily as a husband.

In the dark, the blood smelled
of children I have forgotten to want.
It had seeped from the wedding sheet,
flooded the green-gold box,
climbed over the latch to the floor,
climbed from the floor into the walls,
and so behind the little cedar door I was not to open,
there was nothing but blood,
blood soaking the room in red,
except that in the center was a box so drenched
that it seemed a heart,
stuck to the flagstones with its own stains.

In it was a scrap of vellum
tangled in the threads of a blue beard,
bluer than forbidding.

The blood had washed my name
from the page.

::

How comes this blood upon the key?

I do not know.
Leave me be.

How comes this blood upon the key?

I do not know.
Go from me.

How comes this blood upon the key?

How should I know such a thing,
a good wife and mute as a brick?
You left me, you were kissing statues
who wept in a wild green wold.
I wanted myself
returned to myself.

There is blood on your little golden key—
marriage-blood,
skeleton-spattered.
Look not on it. It does not matter.

Yes, I meant to leave you. But
I did not. A nameless thing
has no right to walk wide
on the knowing earth.
I am here, the tea is ready,
pale in its pot. The joint-boards
of this house
are still stiff and fast along my arms.

You will leave again,
into jungles of statues mourning,
and I will go down through the cellar again,
with the key in my hands. We have done this
until we were sick with it.

And by night, you will kill me
until you are satisfied:
and by morning I will still wake,

turn down the bed,
find brown eggs and coffee
and oranges with ropy white wisps
still clinging.

After the washing is done,
           I will carry the blood you spilt
           over the shaft of the key
down to the little cedar door
in a bucket of wood and iron,
and the little room will strain at the lock.

We will bargain with the white walls
to let us forget how often
we have done these things.

With two blue hands like naked grasping,
you shut me up into this house,
and I have never left it.

An Intersection of Blood and Gold

Parados

First, her hair was black, not gold.
It fell over her shoulders, yes—
dark as mussel-bound shoals—
but her breasts stubbornly refused to be obscured,
refused all that Italian modesty, though she knew
it was well-meant, generously offered.
Her skin was less milk-rose than battered bronze,
her sloping hoplon-belly stitched with stretch-marks
licking flame-slender towards her navel—
the birth of her sons was harder
than their making. Only her daughters
swam easy into the surf.

And him? Old soldier, helmet in hand,
forearms nothing but scars and port-bought tattoos,
blood under the fingernails. He beats his skin
like a carpet, boils the viscera from his ankles,
before he goes in to her. He even slicks his hair
with lemon oil—but he would not admit to it
in the high-terraced hall.
He has broken his knees so many times
he feels his mother's mood swings in the joints.
His left thumb was chewed off in Syracuse.

His chest is covered
in a map—his Corinthian sternum separates
Piraeus from Peloponnese. When he pulls away from her,
sweat-stuck pigment streaks her back
green and blue and golden.

She reclines; he pulls up his body around her,
a tired, needful shell, hard and shining,

and she remembers Cythera,
how her conch-stair was slippery with foam,
how she had to clutch the horns of it
to keep from capsizing.

Their belts hang together on the bedpost,
gold-scale and goat-leather.

Episode

Her hair curls into Ionian waves
when it is wet. Tonight
it smells like lavender and oranges,
though he hates that brand of shampoo.

It is winter. Her scalp steams.
She makes cherry-blossom tea in a white pot.
He tries to touch the nape of her neck,
under a green silk robe.

She shrugs off his fingers.
Her day is a dance to avoid
his hands. She slips aside,
searches the kitchen
for cream.

The bathroom still smells of blue paint;
a silver latch on the cabinet is broken.
She kicks it closed, fishes in the drawer
for a new razor.

"Let me," he says.

Chorus

They have had six children, but in the gilt-ceilinged hall,

it's still called an affair, a scandal—
a flirtation, and who could expect better of her?
As for him, none of us would say she is not beautiful,
the streaks of her stomach, even, comprise
a kind of skin-pale calligraphy.

Her eyes are thickly lined in black. To say she is feline
 is to repeat a dozen hymns and odes to other women, yet,
if he narrows his eyes, he can almost see the spotted pelt,
the slitted pupils. She rolls over,
one knee bent up at an architect's perfect angle.

A golden net—this is the story, isn't it? The only one
they are granted. The only one the vases tell
with their orange-jet tongues. A golden net.
They hardly feel it,
the tinkling, spangled fall.
They are not surprised.

"He is always watching," she sighs.

The weight of it: less than singing
but they cannot lift it with four arms.
It tents over her knee, thatching down
to the bed of olivewood and ram-fleece.

They wait. The dark
sews net to skin.
No one comes to shame them.

Episode

The mirror fogs;
he fills a deep silver bowl.
Hot water, peach soap.

She watches him curiously,
sitting naked on the bathtub-edge.
Her breasts are high and small:
she has had no children. He

is unsure: a leg is not a chin.
His brown hand is quiet on her calf:
ten years practice in the school
of touching her. He lathers her
to the knee, braces her dry foot
against his chest.

"Why are you doing this?" she asks softly,
the new tile echoing.

"It is an act of your body
I have not performed before.
Isn't that enough?"

He draws the razor up in one long stroke,
slightly wobbling,
like the first stalk of the *A*
in a child's primer.

Chorus

They have made love for the third time
under the chime-gold of the net. He curls an arm
almost all the way around her torso,
pushing his legs against the backs of her thighs,
twisted gash-scars pulse purple.

"I don't want him to touch me," she whispers.
"Desire is not indiscriminate.
I try to bear it, but his fingers crawl,
mewling, begging. Worm-hands, trying to

get inside me, always inside.

And he thinks if he drapes enough necklaces
over my throat, enough belts and rings
and skirts and crowns,
I will be in his arms half the creature
I am in yours. And I keep hoping

if he drops enough opals
directly into my navel, if he beats enough
breastplates to the shape of my torso,
enough greaves to my calves,
I will have enough armor
to suffer his hands on me."

"I know," he says,
and strokes the small of her
dolphin-back.

"I remember the green sea
sluicing through crystal lungs,
a shell cold and salty under my lips.
I am a body of foam and water—
why did they give me to a man
who hides under a mountain
and couples with stone?"

"I have no more answer
than the other thousand times
you have asked this thing."
He moves his hand once more
between her myrtle-legs.

Her eyes slant net-ward.
"He and I
are never etched

on the same vase."

She opens under
her red-mouthed soldier.

Episode
He rinses the peach-foam from her leg.
She presents the other foot, but never smiles.
She knows his hands on her
so well that she can no longer
feel them at all.

He draws the silver blade up her calf again,
more sure, now. The long expanse of skin
is easy, but he falters at the crook of the knee,
the razor slips,
a well of blood rises,
wet, carnelian, gleaming in the fluorescent light.

They both watch it swell up,
trickle slowly,
drip onto the bathmat,
blood and soap and steam,
redder than grief.

Chorus

The morning sun, bright as a blood-drop,
turns the net to rubies.
They have fallen asleep, his helmet
still on the shelf.

When they wake, the golden mesh
is no more than a thin blanket:
they pull it over their shoulders,
fold it carefully, like laundrywomen

pressing a wide sheet.

He leaves, rinses the lemon from his hair
thoroughly, so his men do not smell it.
He touches her face before he goes,
his hand huge and rough on her scallop-cheek.

"I will not say
you should have been my wife.
I am not strong enough
to give voice to such a thing.
But you should never
have been his."

The air is cold on his horses' noses.

Aphrodite enters her house
on feet shod in her husband's work:
silver shoes with soles of clicking jasper.
He is asleep still, all the lamps lit,
an iron chain half-worked in his fist.

She lays a golden bundle
on the table by his feet,
softly, softly,
so as not to wake him.

In the grey-shouldered dawn,
she begins to draw a bath.

Exodos
They drink the pinkish tea in separate rooms
and do not speak while turning down
the bedclothes
like old pages.

It is a long time before she comes to bed.

They lie side by side,
as if another body,
shadow-slim and dour,
had slipped between them.

An Issue of Blood

Just then a woman who had been subject to bleeding for twelve years came up behind Him and touched the edge of His cloak. She said to herself, 'If I only touch His cloak, I will be healed.' Jesus turned and saw her, 'Take heart, daughter,' He said, 'your faith has healed you.' And the woman was healed from that moment.

Matthew 9:20-22

Iscah, what is that on your chair?

A few drops, red as accusations—
I hadn't even noticed. I always thought
menarche would sound like weeping, would
feel like a wound opening. But

I never felt the blood come.

The door to my *niddah*-landscape creaked open:
slick, clotted continents crossed
by black rivers afloat with unborn children,
lurid, pitch-sticky inland seas,
mountains of pink limbs, piled up like pyramids,
a spider-clutched geology of impurity.
I slipped inside
and I have never left.

Iscah, what is that on your dress?

I waited for the blood to stop.
I checked my cloths every morning:
that day, surely, I could begin to be called clean.
The cow was bellowing out
her swollen udder,
and she liked no one so well as I.

My legs kept wet and red,
stuck thigh to thigh.
At the end of seven days,
I cut my fingernails, my toenails,
I cut my hair, washed my face,
cleaned my ears. I tucked my hands
into my lap. I waited.
I waited.

But there was no *mikvah*
clear or sweet enough
that I could not turn it
to offal and churn.

Iscah, what is that on your bed?

For twelve years my glass womb broke,
smashing against the *niddah*-shore,
and I could not stop it,
I could not help it,
it ran down my legs
and specked the dust below me:
ash-winged vultures followed my skirts,
pecking at the trail.

Iscah, what is that on your hem?

I touched him. Yes, I touched him—
after twelve years, I wondered
what it would be like to touch a man again.
Just the hem of his cloak, a little
frayed and dirty, no one would notice
my unclean hand
in the road-mire clinging to his heels.

I didn't feel the blood come;

I didn't feel it stop.

But his voice rang out like a stain:

Who has touched me?

I cringed, I hid. *What is that
on your hands, Iscah? What is that
on your sewing? What is that
on your apron? What is that,
what is that,
what is that?*

It is me, and I am red,
and I am wet,
and I am impure,
and what else should I have done?

He stopped, his head ringed
in my vultures
circling high above
his whispering throng.

Iscah, have you touched my cloth?

Yes. For twelve years, I have suffered
an issue of blood.

*I, too, Iscah, have suffered.
An issue of light. It streams out
behind me—it specks the dust.
Bone-winged doves follow my hem
pecking the trail.*

Perhaps
we have stopped up the other's fissures

under this red sun.

Perhaps
our issue will now come as we bid it:
three days of blood
running down the woodgrain
three days of light-flux
scouring the street,
three days of niddah
before we can rest.

His shoulders were very broad
as he turned away from me.

No one would look at me afterwards—
but I am used to that. He took the winding
path down to the salt-sea,
and my vultures followed him.

In my own white walls
I drew a clear bath. I cut my hair,
my fingernails, my toenails.
washed my face,
cleaned my ears. I tucked my hands
into my lap. I scraped
the dried blood from my legs
like a palimpsest,
and sank into the water.
I waited.
I waited.

Iscah, what is that in your bath?

It sloshed over the bronze barrel,
splashed steaming onto the floor,
light like weeping

flushed from me:
bright oil on the surface of the water.
I thought it would sound like singing,
like a wound closing. But

I never felt it come.

Tale Type 6(n-1)3: Red Stockings

Among the seafaring peoples of a certain country, there are no tales of marriage. This is not to say that they do not marry, but that their folklore features none of the traditional narratives of courtship and pair bonding. Their weddings are silent, solemn affairs with very few words and no witnesses, whereas divorce is a lavish ceremony with the full extended family present and a great feast, for only then has the couple achieved maturity. Folktales which treat with the subject at all invariably begin upon the dissolution of marriage. It has been speculated by Drs. ——— & ——— that this situation arose from the high attrition rate of husbands in naval cultures. The following was told to them by a widow in a red dress, with clover in her hair.

  Once there was a woman who had fallen out of love with her husband. Each day she wore more and more red, in order that he should know her heart had changed. Red stockings, red shoes, a red cap, a red skirt, a red shirt, red jewels at her throat, a coat all of red and lined in red as well. Her husband saw this but would not let her go. "If you desire to leave me you must make certain I am warm in your absence. Spin me a year's worth of wool and I will grant what you wish." And so the woman bent to her wheel and spun until her fingers bled—and so she spun for him crimson thread that hurt his eyes. When the spools crowded their house from every corner, her husband said: "If you desire to leave me you must make certain I am fed in your absence. Bake me a year's worth of bread and I will grant what you wish." And so the woman set to threshing their fields with a great scythe, and crushing the wheat and kneading the dough, and in slicing the bread she cut herself, and so baked him great crimson loaves which hurt his throat. But when their larder bulged and wept "No more!" her husband still said: "If you desire to leave me you must make certain I am loved in your absence. Find me another wife as sweet and soft as you and I will grant what you wish." The woman puzzled over this for a long while, and could not think of a solution, for none of the other women in her village wished to wed a man whose wife was so determined to leave him.

Finally, a certain winter morning came, and the husband woke to find a new woman in his bed: crimson loaves shaped into limbs and lips and wrapped in crimson thread, sweet bread and soft cloth, silent and unmoving as the old woman had been for years. His wife had gone in the night, assured that he was warm and fed and loved. He fell to his knees on the threshold of their house, and though he tried not to hear it, the sea-wind brought to him her laughter, and her joy.

Anatomy of a Yes

I don't know how to compete with her—
the one who came
            first.
I was born into the wasteland of her absence,
and elephants have never forgiven me.

I am a stepmother here. The peacocks and leopards
snub me, their black eyes had grown accustomed
to reflecting her narrow face, her swarthy, thorn-stitched hair.
I have tried to explain to the musk-ox
why my mouth is pink, why my hair smells of hyacinth
and not cacao-beans.

He snorts; his breath is hot and wet on my cheek.

Even you—I can hear it,
when you swing my legs over your shoulders
under the baobabs, the shape of her name
behind mine. You grin, brush
a strand of hair from my eyes—
ask if I wouldn't like to go down to the river
and streak it black with fragrant mud.

Only the snake would talk to me. The cottonmouth,
his tongue dart-quick. Only he
did not ask after her, how she fared,
if she would like him to bring her berries
or the corpses of mice.

He told me my hair was pretty.

How was I to refuse?
I was made only to say yes.
Yes, my husband, I want to be kissed.

Yes, you are strong enough to push me
into the clay and the loam.
Yes, I want to grow fat with sons.
Yes, I am dazzled by you, like a lizard
baking her belly in the sun.
Yes, I want an apple—it is so shiny, after all,
and so red.

I am a clockwork woman ticking away—
yes, yes, yes.
She was sewn into the sand for a no,
the skulls of her leather-winged babies
dashed against the mesas.
Even a newborn knows the rhadamanthine law:
this tongue may only taste the skin-crisp of assent.

And now, scrambling in the gorse-brush,
squatting in our grass hut,
I whisper over the swollen belly I have earned,
words the jackdaw taught me,
the prayer you urge me to send up,
to keep her by the beach of crushed bones
that borders the Red Sea:

Senoy, Sansenoy, Semangelof.

Among my thousand yes-syllables,
the names of angels float. But
silent as owls, I wish that she would come,
with her ash-hair streaming,
she who alone is clean of apple-grime
and snake-skin,
and teach me the immaculate word
that bought her black wings
and a far-off desert.

Notes Left by a Previous Tenant

*We used to keep cobalt glasses in this cabinet
and the Christmas mugs.*

We lived here.
You walk and sleep and eat
covered in our dust.

*We let a blackberry cobbler
sit too long in this refrigerator—
it took an hour to scrub
the white dish
white again.*

You stand
in a burning circuit of air,
where I used to stand,
drinking coffee by the bay window—

*I used orange-scented soap;
he used eucalyptus—
you can still smell the soaprings
on the green sink in the hall. He used to say
I smelled like winter,
like winter fruit and rind.*

You read where I read,
by the light of the chandelier
with three bulbs
that flicker in thunderstorms.

*Where the floorboards are still dark,
this was where our bed
put four circles into the wood.
The bed had a name—we named everything*

in this house. We christened the lamps,
the oven, the claw-foot tub.
They are nameless now and yours.

You wash your winter scarves
where I washed mine,
where the soap dried out my hands.
I made goulash on that stove.

You must feel it, the heat
        of skin that is gone.

Crow

The day I left my husband
he turned into a crow.

His black claws chipped the old
cherry-wood footboard, chest-feathers puffed up
Pluto-purpled, indignant. Came his caws:

How dare you? How dare you?

Ten years I slept
with crow-hands on my waist,
washing crow-eggs in the silver sink,
arranging bits of mirror around the bed
so he could watch himself
while his sooty limbs flapped against me.

Once a month, black feathers
sluiced from me like blood.

How dare you? How dare you?

He worried the bedpost
with a dirty onyx beak.
Yolk-slick eyes accused:
it was mine to keep him a man,
to sit alone at a linen-silent table
and polish my love like wedding silver,
knife by knife. It was mine to keep him whole,
to keep him real,
to nail my fingers to the joints
of a house built for the exultation of crows,
to mind my heart like a tea-kettle,
to listen for its wails and scald,
to pour it out at that empty table,

drop by drop into little black cups
like a dull red leaf.

How dare you fail in these things?

Ten years of bookshelves stuffed
with Poe and Hughes,
nest-twigs clotting the closet-hinges,
feathers in the roof-gutters,
my every dress and sleeve dyed black to match him,
ten years of his screeching to the talon-tallied rafters:

How lovely my voice is!
Tell me, tell me how sweet you find my song!

The day I left my husband,
I drew my knees up against my chest,
covered my head with claw-scarred arms.
I know him so well. I know when to raise up my hands.

His jet-throat worked as he leapt:
pecking at my ears, my elbows,
stamping my shoulders bloody.
I fell on the steep black stairs,
fell past black coats hung on hooks, past black hats
and scarves, past black picture frames.
I skidded past black boots and stockings,
black umbrellas barring the door.
His wings beat against my legs,
his cries worked them open—
with the hunger
of a dawn-bird,
he bit into my breasts,
clipped at my lips, scraped scaly toes
against my eyelids. Black feathers
tore out the edges of my jaw,

spilled from my broken mouth
like guilt.

How dare you? How dare you?

In stories ten years is enough:
enough for penance,
enough for service in a land of foreign officials,
enough for rescue, if there is any innocent left
to be lifted out of the dark.
Ten years in the desert, ten years of winter—
it is never enough.

Still I walk under autumn-livid skies,
avoiding the gaze of black birds
still nesting
where our roof once peaked and fell.

Tale Type x + 7:
The Woman of Iron and the Woman of Wood

In a certain remote colony of a certain empire there is a tale which may only be told by sisters to one another. There is a highly ritualized coming-of-age rite by which young girls follow their mothers and their aunts into the forest and spy upon them in the dark, in order to hear the story and tell it among themselves. This is meant to be secretive, but mothers and aunts make sure to have as merry a time as possible, with torches and songs, so that their girls may not lose sight of them in the forest. The whole procession is quite loud and colorful—save for the true secret: the small, dark line of only children who sneak and creep behind, straining to hear just a few words of a story that is forever forbidden to them.

Once there were two sisters, and they were as opposed as a statue with two faces. The elder was a woman grown by the time the younger was born: she was dark and strong as iron, with a serious expression and a love of books. The younger was golden and pliant as new wood, with a bright laugh and a love of roses. The older sister was given away in marriage and went to a far land by the sea which was devoted to the manufacture of gates and closures. There in the country of locks she went into a house and did not come out for many years, until strange news was brought to her by means of a feral cat. The woman of iron bandaged the cat's ear and gave him mice, and the cat told her that in a far land where there was no smell of the sea her sister had disappeared from the house of her father and vanished into a fair forest—none were brave enough to venture after her.

Thus the woman of iron broke the lock of her house and journeyed home. She did not greet her father; she did not embrace her mother. She went straightaway into the fair forest and called her sister's name three times. The woman of wood appeared, surrounded by a wild band of fairies, laughing, chittering like squirrels. Her hair was plaited passing strange, and her skin was spangled with stars, her gown was as autumn mist and there was a crown upon her head—but her sister could see as only sisters see that her feet bled beneath the fine cloth, and her eyes were sleepless and worn.

"I am your sister," said the woman of iron. The fairies slashed at her face with their claws, and her cheeks were red.

"What use is that to me?" said the woman of wood. "You had gone away before I could cut my own meat. Who are you to me?" The woman of iron came nearer.

"I am your sister," she said, and the fairies howled as they slashed at her breast with their claws.

"I am happy here!" cried the woman of wood. "They took me away from a dreary house full of dishes and taught me to dance! Come and dance with us, quit your books and your dour old face!" The woman of iron held out her arms.

"I am your sister," she said, and the fairies slashed at her iron stomach with their little blades.

"All I know of sisters is the leaving of them," snapped the woman of wood. "You will only disappear again, and I will be alone in our father's house! They will keep me forever and safe."

But the woman of iron took her lost sister into her arms, and kissed her ruined feet, and stroked her golden hair with a bloody hand. And the fairies pulled at the woman of wood, and pinched her, and promised her husbands and kingdoms and endless, endless dances.

"I am your sister," whispered the woman of iron. "I am your sister." She wiped the spangles from the eyes of the woman of wood. "I am your sister, and I will never leave you."

And the woman of wood wept upon her sister's wounds, though the salt in them burned and did not heal, but she bore it well, being of stern, grey stuff, and did not let go her golden sister no matter how the fairies hissed, until six days and nights had gone and they could touch the sisters no more.

The two sisters, as unlike as a statue with two faces, went away from the fairy band, but returned neither to their father's house nor to the country of locks. They went into the fair forest and made their home there, having weddings and birthdays and children enough for six women, and each clove well and true to what was theirs, to their books and their roses and their one-eared cat.

Flax

I. *Alular Quills*

I made this mouth for you,
stopped up with nettle and wax.

I pulled it out of our mother
just like you pulled your wings
out of her
white and silver-stiff.

She was so full of gifts, that day.

She held out her arms to me,
dripping with your pale feathers,
and I did want to, I am not ashamed to confess it,
I did want to be a swan.

But I ran, instead, clutching the mouth
to my breast—
my skin warmed it
until it was soft enough to fit
between my jaws.

II. *Humerus*

I pulled on a dress
of hanging moss and hazel twigs.

I made a cloister of branches;
I shaved a tonsure into my skull.
Huddled in a branch-bound nave,
my kneecaps turned to wood, to stone,
and I crushed the flax for you.

I told no one how she broke
my teeth on the kitchen sink,
how she would not let me eat,
how she split my eyebrow
with her wedding ring.

I told no one how she bent back
my brothers' arms until they snapped
into wings.

With the mouth I chewed silence,
mashed and masticated
into a holy thread,
and with this I sewed your shirts
blue as flax-flowers.
My thumbs bled under the nail,
my fingerprints were ground into blankness,
and I bled, I bled,
how I bled in those days,
but I never said a word.

III. *Marginal Coverts*

I was sleeping when he found me.
I had dropped the flax-shirts
onto a gnarled branch.

He climbed through moon-spattered leaves,
climbed over me,
put a ringed hand over my mouth.

He needn't have bothered.
It was for you I said nothing,
I let him push aside my stone knees like doors,
I tore open under him like a sheet of paper,
and I bled,

I bled onto the cloister-wood
and I did not even cry:
the mouth wasn't made for crying.

I tried not to stumble
as he dragged me up the mountain,
dropping flax-flowers behind me,
a trail of breadcrumbs
for hungry birds.

IV. *Scapula*

I wore a white dress.
You would think I was a bride.

The fire smelled of sage and cedar—
as fires will smell. I burned,
as sisters will burn,
for you.

The skin of my seven-year feet
peeled back like feathers,
black and grey,
floating up to thin clouds
and blue air.

But the flax did not burn.
I held it up: the flax
was more precious than I.
Your white wings beat against me,
like flames,
like fists,
begging me, pleading:
You promised.
You promised.

I promised, I promised my boys—
through the stinging ash,
I stretched my hands, my flax-lashed hands,
and I bent your wings forward
until they snapped into arms.

Only my limbs are wood,
yes, even stone, but not iron—
I cannot come back
good and stronger yet,
from ankles blown red and flaming. I am sorry,
I am sorry
I couldn't bear the fire long enough
to give you back everything.

But I burned
for you—

and I never said a word
when he dragged three babies out of me
and let his horse kick out a fourth,
when he ripped up my hair in long handfuls
and bit my breasts purple and yellow—
I never said a word,
I never said no,
I never told anyone what she did to us,
I made my mouth and I clung to it,
even in the smoke,
even in the fire.

V. *Axillars*

It is years since,
and my house is small,
well-made
for a footless crone.

A neighbor boy shovels out
my threshold when the snow
is too high. My brothers visit:
Christmas, Easter.
They are busy, I know:
college, law firm, seminary.
Soon it will only be letters,
birth announcements,
one birthday card,
signed by all seven.

I take my old mouth out of the cupboard:
we eat without speaking.
The youngest cuts carrots with his left hand,
folds his one pure-pale wing
away from the roast pork.

Gringa

My sister once had an affair in Mexico City—
a professor of politics at *Universidad de los Americas*.
Fashionably sympathetic to the Zapatistas,
casually Marxist,
and not too good a Catholic to sleep with my sister
while his wife was visiting cousins in New York.

That first night he told her
she was a white woman
and he owed her nothing. She protested
she was Italian, but he called her
gringa, and that was that. She was
an imperialist cow who didn't speak Spanish,
and he,
he was an honest worker,
man of the people, fucking an American
just to show her the blue-blooded miasma
of her degenerate passport.

I imagine she must have looked like Kansas to him.
Milk-fat and wheat-heavy, full of broad sunny plains
and just enough rain to turn the land green.

She told me at Easter that once,
when their sheets were tangled up
around her legs like coffee leaves,
he got up to go to the bathroom in the night,
and she saw, for a moment,
through the cracked door—
in the mirror the body of her lover
was the body of a bird,
but also the body of a snake,
with thunder in his wingspan,
and a wet wind on his forked tongue,

and the light in his mouth bubbled the glass.

He came back to her bed, fell onto her,
his feathers like arrowheads,
the serpent in him too obvious,
and the god poured himself into her bones like lime,
into her little pale belly, paunched as a profiteer.

My sister squeezed my hand,
pink and yellow with egg-dye
and curled her hair around her ear
behind her new glasses.

"There's spots in my vision now,"
she said,
"All the time, like I looked too long at the sun."

She sat at her desk all that week,
painstakingly indexing her verbs—
habla, hablo, hablaba, hablara, hable.
He laughed at her,
told her a real woman wouldn't take so long
just to learn a Romance language.

Gringa, gringa he crowed,
come back to bed. It's all you're good at.

If she loved him, he said,
twining her thighs in his coils,
if she loved him, she'd stay in Mexico,
learn to cook *mole* sauce,
take care of his ailing mother, whose hips
had crumbled like pages,
shave her cunt for him,
lay down on a stone bed for him,

flay her heart for him,
stop dying her hair. If she loved him,
she'd stop insisting he leave his wife—
marriage is a fascist plot, anyway,
and why should he punish a good Jalisco woman?

When they came to visit us last Christmas,
he grumbled about the capitalist dogma
of our spangled ornaments,
our 9 pound turkey glistening like a gold-skinned baby,
our soft mezzo-soprano two-part harmony.
He spat after her when she went to Mass.

I stayed behind
to wash the big turkey plate,
and he leaned against the black kitchen counter,
leering at me like an overseer.
He put his hands over mine in the soapy water,
and they were cold as storms.
He whispered in my ear,
his breath full of low clouds.

"Did you know, my people,
they used to sacrifice the prettiest girls
at this time of year?
It's been so long, so long,
but their hearts used to be red as apples
on the temple steps.

It didn't hurt them, it was quick.
It was beautiful, like Mass.

They liked it.

    It takes a long time
to take a person apart, you know.

But they bared their breasts to it,
their nipples were tipped in sunlight,
and the knives went in like lovers."

He touched my hair
which is just my sister's shade,
pressed hard against me,
hard enough
that I felt serpent-feathers
prickle at my spine,
and said:

"You look just like her, you know?"

Suttee

In the Indian epic The Ramayana, Sita, a beautiful foundling who was born from a furrow in a lentil field, is the wife of the hero Rama, and is kidnapped by Ravana the demon king, who has fallen in love with her, a parallel to the Greek Persephone story. Unlike Persephone, however, Sita spends years in the demon's enchanted garden, perfectly chaste. When Rama finally rescues her he accuses her of adultery with Ravana, which she denies. He forces her to undergo a trial by fire to prove her innocence, which she survives.

I.

I have a sister.
Her body is made of corn.

Her eyes are apple seeds,
her waist a length of twisted rye.
And when the demon-king came for her,
he burst from the purple cup of the crocus,
and caught her by the grassy heel.

When our mother opened her legs,
my sister's head emerged first,
blonde hair matted with grapes
crushed against that muddy placenta
and olive-meat spattering her skin like henna ink.

I came second from the furrowed earth,
mouth stopped up with sugar and barley—
and such black hair, curled tightly around
my sister's fists.

When it was my turn, a golden deer leapt into a field
and bent its head—the clouds passed like water
over its burnished antlers—to nibble at fallen millet.
The men ran ahead of their spears to catch it,

and I was alone
when the ten-headed demon Ravana
seized my braid like the lead of a dun cow,
and dragged me into the jeweled alleys of Lanka.

I sat on a red silk pillow
in the garden of the scab-haunched king.

She sat on a black throne, and the three-headed dog
dropped asphodel at her feet like meaty bones.

I watched the garden change,
and did not move when I was called
to a black bed with eight posters.

Plums swelled up like bruises,
giving way to persimmons, orange as hanging lanterns,
and withered brown pomegranates, which
knowing those bloodied heart-seeds all too well,
I did not touch.

Snow covered the spiky pines,
and when oranges burned through the ice
an army of silk-snouted monkeys
and men in horned armor
came clamoring through the fruit.

II.

I did not go into the fire for him.

When the wing-footed boy came for my sister
in her wedding gown of peach-skins
she could not hide the red juice
dribbling down her thighs—
but no one called her a whore.

No one waggled their fingers inside her
to inspect the trailing spider-web of her hymen.

They ignored her mouth, loosened
with fruit and weeping.
They came marching down the shadowed stair
and told her to dress herself.

They were understanding—as all officials are—
but they did not let her go.

My husband built me a pyre.

His army of apes piled cedar on cypress
on camphor and rosewood.
The stink of it pricked my eyes.

If you are pure, he said,
the fire will not touch you.
Then I will know.

The monkeys cackled and struck stone on stone,
shrieking at the yellow spark.

III.

I have a sister.
Her body is made of corn.

She would never have survived the fire.
Her amaranth calves would have gone up
like burning books.
And anyway, she is dead.

The demon-king touched his lips to her fingers—
her flesh froze blue and black.

He put his mouth to her navel—
her lips burst open like the mouth of a drowned woman.
And in this body, with all her grains rotted away,
she is wed for half the year.

It was for her I performed *suttee*,
for her I lay my body down
on the fragrant fire, over her cold corpse,
the one who could not get free.

Like a witch I fed the flames.
The sapphires strung through my hair
boiled and bubbled, trickling
into my eyes. I felt her round shoulders,
her slim arm around my waist,
each of her fingers a scald of purity.

All he saw was my gaze turned upwards,
the mandala of fire.
All he saw was my skin still whole,
my bones uncharred,
my hips smooth and cool.

IV.

I crawled back into my loamy mother,
hemorrhaging children.

He followed behind, stuffing our sons
into a reed basket, protesting loudly—
he believed me, now. He knew
I was chaste as an infant dove.

But he cannot find the opening.
Through the clay and the mud, I crept
into the furrowed earth and drew up my knees

to my chest. In the dark of my mother's body,
I sleep.

In the spring, my sister wriggles in beside me,
and curls my hair—such black hair!—around her fists.

Tale Type 17894:
The Stalwart Historian

There is a story which the books in certain libraries tell one another when the librarian has turned out the lights and gone home to soup and kettle. This would have remained a secret but for a student who fell asleep in one of these libraries and was not glimpsed by the cleaning staff on their final rounds, and so awoke past midnight with pages in a stir all around her, whispering periodical to encyclopedia, index to glossary.

Everyone knows a library is a forest. Oak and ash and hawthorn and fir, closed up in cowhide, closed up in shelves, closed up in a great house. It should be unsurprising, then, that every so often a young historian on a quest becomes entangled here, and it is our lot to help or hinder, depending on what we have had for breakfast that morning. It happened this way once, a poor paladin tasked by terrible black-masked masters to return to them the fruit of the truth-telling plum-tree. She went first to the dictionaries, but they were deeply and alphabetically apologetic, having never been plum-trees.

"Try the biographies," they said, and gave her synonyms of invisibility to help her on her way. The biographies were profoundly, genealogically embarrassed, having never been plum-trees, either.

"Try fiction," they suggested, and gave her tragic foreshadowing to help her on her way. Every novel claimed to remember having violet flowers and a long black trunk, but the historian was clever and knew them for liars. They were acutely, dramatically ashamed, and gave her a allegorical blade to help her on her way.

But by this time the young historian was quite lost, and had given up hope of finding what she sought. She sat down heavily upon a stepladder and buried her face in her hands. But in her despair she smelled a sweet scent, like the wind through a long ago plum-orchard in spring blossom. She looked up and spied us on our one lonely shelf, which bears all the truth it can—which is not very much, or else it cries in the night. But we came only to witness. We watched our grim comrade stalk her, we watched her spin around and cry woe, we watched her as she set to her battle in the center of the wood, and the History of the World bore heavily upon her, despite her blade, despite her foreshadow, despite her invisibility. But she swung bravely, and struck true, and saved a slim and tremulous volume of poetry from its depredations, which she took to her home and to her bed, and married in the strange ceremonies of historians after being punished by her masters for her failure to locate us.

For our part we gave succor and bandages and medicines to the History of the World, and restored it to its place, but it has never been the same, and it limps when there is a storm coming in.

The Seven Devils of Central California

I. The Devil of Diverted Rivers

Put out your tongue:
I taste of salt. Salt and sage
and silt—
dry am I, dry as delving.

My fingers come up
through the dead sacrament-dirt;
my spine humps along the San Joaquin—
remember me here, where water was
before Los Angeles scowled through
hills blasted black
by the electric hairs of my forearms.

Pull the skin from my back and there is gold there,
a second skeleton,
carapace smeared to glitter in the skull-white sun.
There is a girl sitting there
between the nugget-vertebrae
who came all the way from Boston
when her daddy hollered Archimedes' old refrain—
Eureka, baby, eureka, little lamb,
I'll have you a golden horse
and a golden brother
and golden ribbons for your golden hair,
just pack up your mama and come on over Colorado,
not so far, not so.

They flooded out her daddy's valley
when she was seventeen,
rooting potatoes out of the ground,
brushing beetles from her apron,
and the wind sounded like an old Boston train.

I am waiting for you to stop in your thrum,
for you to pause and look towards Nevada:
I am holding back the waters
with the blue muscles of my calves,
waiting for you.
All the way down to the sea,
one of these mornings bright as windows,
I'll come running like a girl
chasing golden apples.

I deny you, says the city below.
I deny you, says the dry riverbed, full of bones.
I deny you, say the mute, fed fields far off from the sea.

II. The Devil of Imported Brides

Look here: my fingernails show through
the lace and dried orange blossoms of a dress
I never wore.

You can see them up on the ridgeline like a fence
severed by earthquake:
yellow and ridged, screw-spiraled, broken,
brown moons muddy and dim.

The roots of the Sierras are blue and white:
the colors of stamped letters, posted,
flapping over the desert like rag-winged vultures,
gluey nose pointed east. All around the peaks
the clack of telegraphs echo
like woodpeckers:

Would like a blonde, but not particular.
Must be Norwegian or Swede, no Germans.
Intact Irish wanted, must cook better than the ranch-hands.

Don't care if she's ugly enough to scare the chickens
out of their feathers, but if she ain't brood-ready,
she goes right back to Connecticut
or the second circle of hell
or wherever it is
spit her out.

Look here: my horns spike up sulfurous through
a veil like mist on the fence-posts. My tail rips the lace;
thumps black on the floor of an empty silver mine.
Never was a canary in the dark
with a yellow like my eyes. Sitting
in the cat-slit pupil with her bill of sale
stuffed in her mouth—

Why, hullo, Molly! Doesn't your hair look nice!
If you glisten it up enough
he'll be sure to love you real and true,
not for the silver nuggets you pull out of the rock
like balls from the Christmas box,
not for the crease-eyed boys he pulls from you
like silver nuggets, but for the mole on your little calf,
and the last lingering tilt to your voice,
that remembers Galway.

It was the seventh babe killed her,
and I sat up in her bloody bed,
orange blossoms dead on the pillow,
the clacking of brass-knockered codes
so loud in my ears
I flew down to the mine,
deeper than delving,
just for silence.

It is cold down here,
what silver is left

gnarls and jangles.
I put my hands up through the mountains
like old gloves with their fingers torn,
and wait.

I deny you, says the father of seven, bundled against the stove.
I deny you, says the silver, hanging in the earth
like a great chandelier.
I deny you, say the mountain towns, minding their own.

III. The Devil of Fruit Pickers

Strawberries and nickels
and the sun high as God's hat.
My old callused feet stamp down
the green vines and leaves of Fresno,
my throat of bone whistling still
for water.

My wings are tangled in grapevine
and orange-bark,
pearwood and raw almonds,
 green skin prickles my shoulder blades,
lime-flesh and rice-reeds,
soybean pods and oh,
the dead-leaved corn. I can hardly fly
these days.

But I burrow, and stamp,
and how the radishes go up in my path.

Between the wings rides Maria,
born in Guadalajara with strong flat feet,
fishy little mouth scooped clean
by her father with cheeks like St. Stephen.
This was before the war, of course.

Her black hair flies coarse as broom-bramble,
bags of oranges belted at her waist,
singing while I dance, riding me like her own
sweat-flanked horse.

She saved her nickels, and picked her berries,
bent over,
bent over,
bent over in the fields till her back was bowed
into the shape of an apple-sack,
and nothing in her but white seeds and sunburn.
She curled up into me,
dry as an old peapod,
and how we ride now,
biding our time,
over the dust and cows,
over all her nickels in a neat bank-row.

Watch our furrows, how we draw them,
careful as surveyors,
careful as corn-rows.

I deny you, say the strawberries, tucked tight into green.
I deny you, say the irrigation ditches, glimmering gold.
I deny you, say the nickels, spent into air.

IV. The Devil of Gold Flake

My hair runs underneath the rivers,
gold peeling from my scalp. I remember
the taste of a thousand rusted pans
pulling out ore like fingernails at the quick.

I lie everywhere;
I point at the sea.

All along my torso are broken mines,
like buttons on a dress. The state built
a highway through them,
a grey rod to straighten my back. The driller-shacks
shudder dusty and brown,
slung with wind-axes and bone-bowls:
my stomach dreams of the ghosts of gold.

They suck at my skin,
hoping for a last gurgle of metal,
tipping in for the final bracelet and brick—
there must be something left in me,
there must be something—why do I not give it to them,
selfish creature, wretched mossy beast?

Underneath the deepest drill
hunches Annabella, the miner's wife,
who sifted more gold
 than her coarse-coated man,
so deft and delicate were her fingers
round that old, beaten pan. He brought her
from St. Louis, already pregnant—and manners
make no comment there—already heavy with gold.
She smelled of the Mississippi
and steam-fat oatmeal cakes,
even after the oxen died, and with blood in her hair,
she crossed half of Wyoming on foot.

But the boulders loved her,
watched her every day from a high blue perch.
They wriggled at her, her yellow dress
gone brown with creek-silt, her bustle
and wire hoops collapsed on the grass.
While she knelt with gold in her knuckles,
they snapped to attention,
slid laughing to the creek-bed—she doesn't blame

the poor things, even now.
Her babies left cabbages and peppermints
at the creek for years after.

I felt the highway roll smooth and hot
over my ox-drenched head,
and the only gold I allowed to ooze up from my scalp
were the broken dashes marking lanes
like borders on an old map
showing a river like a great hand flattening the page.

But I confess:
I am an old wretched beast, and my tail,
waiting in the spangled dust,
is made of quartz-shot boulders
clapped in moss.

I deny you, say the desiccated lodes.
I deny you, say our great-grandchildren, with such clean hands.
I deny you, says the highway, blithe and black.

V. The Devil of Mine Canaries

Watch the sun peek out over the Siskiyous
with their lavish snow like ladies' bonnets—
see my feathers, how bright, how brave!
I open my wings over the thin green
boyish arms of the Russian River,
yellow as sulphur, yellow as gas,
wide as any Italian angel.

What is a devil
but death and wind?
I come golden as a mineshaft,
and how black, how ever black,
come my eyes!

Who remembers where they got the songbirds?
Bought from Mexico, from Baja with shores
like sighs? They got the cages
out of their wives' bustles, wrangled
to hand and wing. *Pretty bird, pretty bird!*
Don't be afraid of the dark.

Yella-girl loved her miner, thought
her black demon,
white eyes showing clam-shy through the dust,
was the greatest raven born since Eden.
She pecked corn-meal from his palm,
stood guard at his bedknob,
little golden sentinel. She'd draw the gold
for him, she thought, like to like.

For birds, the angry gases
have a strange color:
pink, almost pretty (Pretty bird, pretty bird!)
curling up from the dark like beckoning.
Yella-girl seized up in mid-stroke,
falling onto a carpet of jaundiced feathers
half a leg deep. She fell thinking
of her miner, of corn in his black hand,
and I stood up
out of the canary-grave,
body crawling with pretty, pretty birds,
beaks turned out
like knives.

I deny you, says the buried mine, long stopped up.
I deny you, say the crows, too big to tame.
I deny you, says the miner, a new bird swinging at his side
like a lunchbox.

VI. The Devil of Acorn Mash

I am hard to see.
You will have to look carefully.

Carefully down,
at your well-shod feet
to see the shallows in the rock,
where she and her son,
light beating their black hair like blankets,
worked rough-husked black oak acorns
into mash and meal,
bread and pancakes.
Like horse-hooves driven into
the granite, the hollows still breathe.

These are my footprints.
I have already passed this way
and gone.

I deny you, says the forest, full again.
I deny you, say endless feet.
I deny you, says the treeless plain, flat and brown.

VII. The Devil of the Railroad

If I just try, I can taste bitter tang
of the golden tie bent over my toe
somewhere in Kansas,
like the memory of licking clean a copper plate.

But here at my head,
between the Santa Lucias and two crescent bays,
ribboned and raw-boned, bonneted in iron,
coal-shod and steam-breathed, I taste
corn-freight and cattle, palettes of tomatoes

and stainless steel screwdrivers, and there, behind my tongue,
the phosphorescent traces
of silver forks and weak tea shaking on linen,
burning the air where they no longer
drink themselves down to calm nerves like baling wire,
to spear Pacific salmon before the conductor ever sighted blue.

Out of the slat-cars come thousands of horns,
honest black and brown,
bull-thick, tossing in the heat.

In the slick, wet turn of my silver-steel against the rail
Li-Qin sings a little song, full of round golden vowels.
She wore gray shapeless things, hammering ties,
taking her tooth-shattering turn at the drill,
laying rail with bloody, sun-smashed hands
while the pin against wood sounded her name over and over
like a command to attention:
Li-Qin, Li-Qin, Li-Qin!
She had tea from thrice-used bags
and a half bowl of rice at the end of the day,
one grain of sugar dissolving in her cup
like snow.

With her hair bound back she plied the drill
until it slipped like splashed water,
hammered into her heart,
laying track for the train to bellow through her,
blood red as cinnabar on the wooden stays.

There is a car swinging back and forth
between a shipment of umbrellas to San Francisco
and swordfish packed in ice for Santa Barbara.
I have such a tail, you know, enough to bring them all
from the mountains and the sea.
With silver forks and weak tea

they sit at a long table with a cloth of cobwebs,
clinking their cups as I rattle them through the desert:

a Boston goblin with drowned lips violet,
a bridal imp, her veil torn and burning,
a gnomish grandmother, sucking tea through slices of strawberries,
an old, wretched, bustleless beast, smug as a river,
a yellow bird, brimstone-wings folded around
a little urchin in deerskin, her hands full of acorns,
and a demon in gray with a huge flayed heart
hanging in her breast like a pendant.

I brought them on my tail,
my endless black tail,
like a dragon out of books older than any of us,
I brought them like freight,
like wagons,
like horses,

and we are coming to dance on the shore
by the great golden bridge,
we are coming to remember ourselves
to the tide,
to sing at the moon until it cracks,
to stamp our hooves under so many crinoline dresses,
to stamp our hooves under so many rags,
to stamp our hooves on the earth like pickaxes,
and sunder California along every wrinkle,
send her gleaming
into the sea.

I deny you, shudders the sky, whole and inviolate.
I deny you, whispers the unwilling sea.
I deny you, trembles the fault line.

The sun dips deep into salt and foam,

and a long engine-whistle
breaks the blue
into seven pieces.

Lessons in Thermodynamics

There is a story I want to tell you.
It begins:

Once the gods alone had joy of Fire.

On bolts of iron they kept her bright,
laid together like a ladder down
to plains of ash and coke
or a bed
whose slats bruised the thin volcanic air.
Their beards were singed,
the greycurl of smoking oil filled every hall,
lemonseed, and balsam, and green galangal.

On a copper cart they brought her weeping flame
into their banquets of goose-bones
wrapped in ox-fat.
She burned for them,
red of mouth,
red of lobe,
red of spleen,
rolling on the scorched bolts,
rolling beneath their hands—
a palm on her stomach that smelled of the sea,
a thumb under her tongue tart as blood,
a knuckle like an unripe grape at the base of her throat,
fingers falling like wheatseeds on her embers of her nipples.

I remember this
as a painting in sinopia and clay
depicting in black figures
a thing done
to somebody else.

But it was my navel
into which the drunkard and the owl
spat olive-pits. Mine too
the hair they cut
to light the stairwells back
to antechambers
where the sea thrust into the willing moon
and the walls were washed in blue.

Trickster, take me.
Trickster, cut me loose.
I will burn such things
for you. I will show you
such incandescence.

But he lay on his chaise,
his eyes rolled back
in *kykeon*-stupor, barley
spilled over his chest.

Trickster, take my hands
in your hands.
Trickster, hide me fast.
I will set the world on fire for you.
I will burn the black heaven white.

Even ears stuffed with clay and ginger
will sometimes hear.
Trickster took me up
from the bed of the sun
where his golden arms
clamped me jealously,
hungrily in—
fire is after all,
inarguably within
the circles of the sun's strength.

Trickster tucked me in his coat
and shushed me among
the sleeping shavings of the cosmos.

How tall he was, they will tell you:
Prometheus descending
the rhodite stair of heaven,
with fire in his hands
for the joy of men.

You know what happens next,
do you not? It is an old story, after all.

But I was young. I had not
yet heard it.

To every camp he took me
crowned in coal and fawnskin
he pulled me,
red of palm,
red of tongue,
red of knees.
With a rope of wild grasses
he lashed and leashed me,
and in the centers of those camps,
he struck my spine
a fist at the base,
an elbow round my throat.

Again he struck,
and a third time,
like an eagle
prying lichen from stone.

And into the ground
I retched flame,

I wept fire.

Trickster, hold me by the hair,
tell them how to say your name
with all due awe.
Look how they watch for us
to crest the hills of their home.
How like morning we are,
how like a star.

I lay down beneath him;
I crawled on my belly.
When he left me for the gold-clawed eagle,
I lay in pieces over frozen mud
and grassland
and stone plain.

It was cold;
ashes wheeled.

There is a story I want to tell you.
It ends:

In this manner was Fire brought to the world.

Red shows through the skin of the world
in every crack and fissure.

Trickster, tie me down.
Trickster, close my mouth.
You cannot let me free
in all my many limbs.
I will grow, as bodies do.
I will reach out more fingers
than there are gods on high seats,
and in the furrows I dig

there will be heat and death
enough to swallow
all the depthless skies.

Tale Type 00:
The Last Story of Urn

In the salt-marshes of a particular lowland country, there is a story which old women tell on their deathbeds. They spend their lives practicing for this moment, rehearsing it, planning for the accompanying flute and drum, carefully removing and adding words to their variant. The name of the protagonist is constant, and a popular character in other folktales of the region. The telling is a great event for which all her loved ones are present, a bed placed out of doors so that it slowly sinks into the marshes as the old grandmother's thin and raspy voices carries over her rapt audience. The following was recorded in 19— by two young researchers who had a distant relationship to the deceasing, something less than nieces and more than cousins.

 Once there was a woman called Urn, who in her youth was merry and beautiful, and married many a dragon and slayed many a prince. She had her children, she planted her gardens, she baked her cattail-cakes. When her children had their children, when her husbands were all buried and she was grown old and wrinkled as good bark, she was restless, and went into the forest to seek her fortune. She took with her a grass bow and a quiver of strong arrows, and ate well by their fruits. She had many adventures in the wood, beset by serpents and lions, saints and suitors: her arrows pierced them all.

 One evening she came upon a high and spindly house, not a tower, but a house so tall and thin one could only pass through the door sideways, and could not see the roof at all, lost in the clouds. She fired a friendly arrow into a window-shutter, and a tall, thin man peeked out at her, clothed all in grey.

 "Good evening, old woman," he said.

"Good evening, old man," she answered, and was admitted for supper to the spindly house. There she offered him her day's kill, and he offered her a goblet of blood, which she sipped only diplomatically. With her lips still red the thin man tried to kiss her, but she rebuffed him.

"Stay with me, Urn, and be my lover. This house is your house, this blood is your blood."

"I have had my fill of lovers and houses and blood," Grandmother Urn answered, and went to sleep in a tall, thin bed.

But she liked the grey man, and stayed, hunting on his grounds with her grass bow and riding his thin grey horses. And at dinner each night the man coaxed her to tell stories of her life, which piled up between them like meat. And he would ask her to be his lover, and she would laugh. Finally, when over her venison and his blood she told the tale of finding the tall, thin house, the man came to her and lay his head upon her lap and said:

"Urn, yield to me, for I love you and you are fair. Stay with me and be my love, this house is your house, this blood is your blood, this creature is your creature."

And Grandmother Urn knew that she did love the tall thin man in his tall thin house, and put her arms around him like one of her own babes, and kissed him, and took him to her bed, this creature who was called Death, who had waited faithfully for her all her life.

Past the Rivers

I sat as if a statue,
and Hades brushed my hair
with a comb of iron and asphodel.

I sat as if an icon,
and Demeter brushed my hair
with a comb of crocus and water.

On either side of my candled body,
they held out my hair like wings,
and ran their fingers through it,
oars through black and separate rivers.

And Hades' hand was on my knee, saying:

You are safe here,
where we have brought you.

And Demeter's arms were close on mine, saying:

We only meant the dark
to be a quiet pool
where we can whisper
and remain unheard.
The sky is so bright, and so brazen.

I still clutched shreds
of daffodils and crabgrass in my fists,
and warm salt-sweat
drawn from the well of the sun
lingered in my lashes. My shoulders,
still,
were rosed with sunburn.

*You would have squatted bent-knee
on an island in the sea
and lightning-infants
would have torn out of you
in blue arcs. Your stretch marks
would have been jagged as thunder,
so wide,
and so white.*

And oh, they lay me down among the poplars,
the stalks glower-white,
white as standing corpses.
And oh, their voices were steam
rising from black and separate streams.

*We brought you past the rivers
where no lightning falls.
The trees here are whole—so tall,
and so white.*

I closed my eyes—it made no difference
in the dark. Over one half of me
she lay wheat warm as scarves;
over the windward side,
he draped shrouds thin as gasping

In the corners of the shadows,
I heard the sound of blackbirds passing.

They let my hair fall,
and it covered my skin like a dress.
His hand was shadow;
her hand was corn-light gleaming,
and in each they held out to me

      a blaze of wet, red fruit.

The Immigrant

The cats have gnawed away
the white paint of the window pane—
through their teeth-marks the snow
is impossibly cold. Old light falls on the freeze
like long, blue bones. I didn't know
snow could be like this:
so bitter and bleak under the black,
dry and hard as dead skin.

You are so thin on the bedsheets,
thinner than anyone else I've brought here.
Your stubble is a forest of tiny shadows
in the windowlight. You are young as birch,
barely twenty, and I tell you like a confession:

        Baba Yaga was young once, you know.

You laugh like a crow perched on my bedpost:
        How do you know?

Born in Murmansk, you know everything.
I am just an American girl
with needle-green eyes and three cats—
what could I know about houses on chicken legs
and cupolas red as the skulls of sons in the dawn?
You like the curve of my hip
as it descends into my leg, certainly,
but this is your world we're talking about,
and I have no passport back
to those black, slantwise crosses,
those close-trunked woods,
that raw pig fat and salted fish you remember.

But she was young. She had hair so golden

it made the tsar cry once. He begged her to
rest within his treasury, with emeralds pressing
on all sides like green hands. She told him
she had pigs to feed.

                        She wore a green apron
like the tsar's emeralds, with goose-beaks
dangling from the strings,
and her cheeks were a little milk-fat,
whipped slap-pink by wind. She owned three
horses. She owned seven pigs with black spots.

You kiss the inside of my wrist.
           You don't say her name right,
you laugh, and I am ashamed.

But her lips were so red. Red as menarche,
red as plague. She did not want the tsar.
She did not want
his silly daughters in their ridiculous hats
pestering her, echoes of their fur-belted father.

It was Sunday when she slaughtered her seven pigs,
one by one with the tip of a reindeer horn.
The churchbells struck the sky like hammers.
It was Tuesday when she made her suitcase,
and folded up into it:
her picket-fence of skulls and femurs,
her mortar and her pestle like a stone oar,
her birch broom dust-clung with snow.

She gave her horses, the red, the white, the black,
three apple cores, brown at the bite-marks,
and slapped their rumps as they trotted obediently
past the latches and straps.

She shook out a trail of corn from her apron-pocket
to entice her peak-roofed house into the bag.
It came hesitantly,
sniffing the air with its chimney,
hen-claws scrabbling back and forth,
closer, closer.

Baba Yaga closed her valise with a snap
like toes breaking.

> I must be very careful
> with what I tell you next.
> I put my chin to your shoulder and speak
> as slowly as a grandmother.

In New York,
they wrote down her name in a big book,
big enough to belong
in the library of Koschei the Deathless:
Barbara Young.
She blinked. It was not a name she knew. It was not
her name. Her house
creaked mournfully in her bag.

She settled in Ohio, in a forest with tall, thin birches
like fingers stuck in the soil. Her hair still peeked out,
golden-white, from a kerchief
at the meat-rendering plant
where she worked, cleaning all those bones to white,
all those bones, all those pretty skulls.
She had children, twins, and a daughter after,
and she did not tell her husband, the meat-foreman
with a beard like a tsar,
that some cold nights,
when the snow was hard and shrieking underfoot,
she wanted to eat them,

just to stop them squalling, red-faced as pigs.

Girls came, just as before.
Corn-yellow Midwestern girls,
looking for summer work before the fall semester,
willing to sweep out her stoop,
willing to scrub her mortar spotless,
bothering her with questions
about the old country, as if she wants to talk about it,
as if they do not hear
her peak-roofed house growling
like an old woman's stomach.

She didn't keep her fence, though,
            I whisper into the curled bones of your ear.
There are no fences out here;
land blurs into land.
She cut it into grey slats and white rails
to make a bed,
with four posters and a creaking,
marrow-thick frame. On that bed
she kissed a foreman until his lips bled.
On that bed she had three children,
her womb stretching hip to hip. On that bed
she showed her granddaughter
a photograph, gone brown at the edges
like an apple core,
of a young woman in a dark wood,
with hair so golden
it might make a tsar cry.

I put my arm across your waist—so thin,
thin as a woman's. I am so hungry for you,
my throat is open, bright, wet. With
            one gentle hand,
I turn your face,

pointing your gaze
at the foot of the bed.
          Did you not see
             the bedknobs glinting, my love?
Four great eyeless skulls
shine silver in the shadows
the moon throws
on hard, cracked snow.

The Eight Legs of Grandmother Spider

1

I will go,
said a double-jointed voice
out of the dark.

I will fetch the sun
from the country of fire
and bring it back
safe as bread.

In the black,
the only sound
was icicles jangling
on frozen fur.

No,
said the animals,
huddled one against the other,
Possum will go.
He is bigger than you,
and he can hide the sun in his bristle-tail.

Balanced on her basket-web
over the lightless water,
Spider shrugged
and sighed.

2

   I was four—
four, and you were seventy-two,
in your silver wheelchair,
black and green afghan

over corduroyed knees,
with my skinny arms
wrapped around you,
and your hands on my new dress.
I curled into sleep on your knitted lap
breathing your smell
of cinnamon and antiseptic cream.

The TV gurgled lazily,
cartoons and mint toothpaste ads
and my hair was tangled
in the pretty beads around your neck
those tight black curls
and my brown ringlets
twisting to make a second chain.

Both of us snored a little,
soft as cats,
covered in light
like your heavy orange rhododendrons,
light drifting in
through the windows
that would have been washed
when you got around to it.

3

In the black,
the only sound
was Possum
whimpering and licking
his pink tail, scalded bald.

I will go,
said a silk-sticky voice
out of the dark.

*I will fetch the sun
from the other side of the world
and bring it back
safe as swaddling.*

Chattering jaws
gnawed frostbitten bones
and pupils were open pools
in shivering skulls.

No,
said the animals,
groping for purchase
in the shadows.
*Buzzard is cleverer than you,
and besides,
he can fly.
He will balance the sun on his head,
like a woman carrying water.*

Busy wrapping a bee
in gauze,
Spider shrugged
and sighed.

4

You hands were folded over my shoulders,
the hands of a chicken farmer
who wrung the necks of roosters
up north of Talequah for forty years—
        whose mother
was pale enough to pass,
but for that sleek braided hair
and those too-black eyes,

>whose handsome husband

left her with six children,
>>whose red-headed daughters

ran off to Los Angeles together
and came home every night smelling
of movie popcorn and orange soda,
>>whose grand-daughter

was a beautiful actress
and went to a grand university,
>>whose great-granddaughter

was four,
was four,
and still moved her lips when she read.

5

In the black,
the only sound
was Buzzard
cawing and rubbing
his pink head, scalded
to a bald wrinkle.

I will go,
came a thick-bellied voice
out of the dark.

I will fetch the sun
from the land of light
and bring it back
safe as sealing wax.

Horns butted against antlers
against feathers against fins,
so lost were all things
in the murk of the world.

Go, then,
said the animals
since Possum and Buzzard
were burned up like birch bark.
Go, fetch the sun for us,
we are so cold,
and so blind—
the kittens' eyes do not open,
the larvae do not hatch
the chicks do not break their eggs.

Spry on eight grey legs,
Spider shrugged,
and climbed over the shale,
silk drifting behind her.

6

Later my aunts would tell me
that when I was born
You held me first of anyone
and wept over my dark little head.
They said we looked like a photograph
they have of you,
black-haired infant
in the arms of your mother
in the days when she would whisper
when she knew no one would hear:
aquetsi ageyutsa,
aquetsi uwoduhi ageyutsa.

They said my pupils were open pools;
I looked up at you
and your tears splashed
on my cheeks,

that first evening
in the hospital over the sea
when the white sailboats
were tipped in gold
and rocked like a lullaby on the slow water.

You sang to me
in the white walled maternity ward
whispering and crooning—
but it is a only story I have been told
I can't recall your voice,
or what song it might have been.

7

The sun scorched the basket,
of course.

And her legs, not so different
in thickness
from the coffer-straw,
singed at the tips
like used matches.

But for them,
she put the fire
like a bright ball of dough
into the clay,
and it made of the clay a kiln,
and it made of the kiln an oven,
and it made of the oven a womb.

For them,
she melted the ice
from her own small, grey body
and with the sun

like a corn-cake frying beneath her,
she boiled herself
into day,
a little dark speck
dwindling
against the sudden blaze.

8

It was so simple and quiet:
         I woke up
and you didn't.

I was four;
I couldn't understand, quite,
but I started to scream,
babbling for you,
tugging at your hands,
your chicken-throttling hands,
your seed-scattering hands,

your sun-stealing hands.

And all I have of you now
is your nose and high forehead
and this sleek hair,
these too-black eyes—
and how I held you last of anyone,
         that you died in my arms
when I was four years old
and the late afternoon sun
lay in your lap like a baby.

CREDITS

Lessons in Thermodynamics: **Flytrap**, May 2008

The Girl With Two Skins: **Goblin Fruit**, Spring 2008

Crow: **Jabberwocky 3**, November 2007

The Seven Devils of Central California , Rampion, The Immigrant: **Farrago's Wainscot**, Summer 2007

How Comes This Blood Upon the Key, Glass, Blood, and Ash, Inhumed Her Star-Staked Body Bloodless Lies, An Issue of Blood, and *An Intersection of Blood and Gold:* **Grendelsong**, April 2007

Flax: **Goblin Fruit** January 2007

Notes Left by a Previous Tenant: **Xelas Magazine** November 2007

Past the Rivers: **Goblin Fruit** October 2006

The Anatomy of a Yes and *The Inkmaker's Wife:* **Electric Velocipede**, Winter 2006

The Child Bride of the Lost City of Ubar: **The Journal of Mythic Arts**, Fall 2006

The Gardener and the Grave-Keeper: **Cabinet des Fées**, Fall 2006

Pasiphae's Machine: **Heliotrope Magazine**, August 2006

Helen in the Underworld: **Lone Star Stories**, August 2006

Suttee: **Jabberwocky 2**, July 2006

The Frog-Wife: **Lone Star Stories**, Spring 2006

The Eight Legs of Grandmother Spider: **MYTHIC**, Spring 2006

The Descent of the Corn-Queen of the Midwest: **Mythic Delirium**, Summer 2006

The Queen of Hearts: **Mythic Delirium** 2005

Sedna, Submerged: as part of *The Ice Puzzle*, 2004-2005

Skadi in the Forest of Legs: as part of *The Ice Puzzle*, 2004-2005

About the Author

Born in the Pacific Northwest in 1979, **Catherynne M. Valente** is the author of the *Orphan's Tales* series, as well as *The Labyrinth*, *Yume no Hon: The Book of Dreams*, *The Grass-Cutting Sword*, and four books of poetry, *Music of a Proto-Suicide*, *Apocrypha*, *The Descent of Inanna*, and *Oracles*. She is the winner of the Tiptree Award and the Million Writers Award and has been nominated for the Pushcart Prize and the World Fantasy Award, the Rhysling Award, and shortlisted for the Spectrum Award. She currently lives in Northeastern Ohio with her partner, two dogs, and two cats. Her sixth novel, *Palimpsest*, will be released by Bantam Spectra in February of 2009.